#195     10 —

*[Handwritten inscription:]* Julie: Back in 8th grade your bravery inspired me and STILL this story! I hope you enjoy you and your and your lovely family. Much love, Michael Miller

# I SHOULD HAVE WORN PANTIES

Michael Lee Miller

2018
INDEPENDENTLY PUBLISHED
Cover art by Hayley Knighten

# ACKNOWLEDGMENTS

I don't know where to start.

Mom and Dad - Thank you for everything. You inspired most of this story and I wish I could properly show you my appreciation. This will have to do.

Hayley - Thank you for your friendship, love, loyalty, and wisdom. And this dope cover.

Laura - I would not be here, writing these acknowledgments without you. I am grateful for you.

Maddie, Carl, Chrissy, and Lisa - You all have so much more depth than I was able to portray in this book. Your friendships mean the world to me.

Timothy, Paul, and JD - You are my world. DFTBA and know that mommy loves you. Please don't ever read this.

And to everyone else who believed in me and supported me along the way - You ain't seen nothing yet.

Thank you all.

2011 sucked: my mom died, I turned 30, and my husband left me.

None of these events were directly related, nor were they independent. They were, as most things, a complicated, fragile web of cause and effect. Connections woven over time and experience bound by events and memories.

My mother had the saddest life of any person I've ever known. Her family, rocked by the murder of her youngest brother, drank themselves to death before I was born. She followed suit, dragging it over the three decades of my life. It was a painful, arduous finality to a sad life. My grief over the loss of my mother was softened by the end of her misery. People kindly volunteered their condolences, a sympathetic hand on mine: "She's not in pain anymore." They had no idea how much truth and weight invisibly filled their sentiments.

I was offered similar platitudes after my divorce, just nine months later. Arms wrapped around my shoulders, encouraging me to make the most of my new freedom. I was polite. I smiled and nodded hopefully, granting them the absolution of care they secretly craved. The unspoken truth of the split: I was fucked. An at-home-mom of nearly a decade, I had no work experience or education. For those doing the math, I was a young mom. Not exploitable-on-MTV young, but I was in no way ready for motherhood either.

I did what I was expected to do: cut my hair into a spunky style and hit the pavement with my freshly printed, inflated resumes. I got a terrible job selling crappy internet service, commission only. I think I made about $400 my first and only month with that company. I then decided to mooch off the government with a Pell Grant, sent in my FASFA and enrolled at the local community college. I had no educational plan other than paying my mortgage and scheduling my classes around my children's needs. They'd only known a mom that was 100% available to them and I wasn't ready to change even more in their lives. As heartbroken was I felt, I could only imagine their pain.

They're great kids. Yes, every mother says that, but in my case it's actually true. Smart, charismatic, courageous shitheads with big mouths and giant hearts. My former husband, James, and I agreed to an amiable, friendly divorce to make it as easy as possible for the children. We politely co-parent and didn't wage war over the worthless furniture or broken promises. On the surface, my children only saw a brave, hopeful divorced mom.

Inside, I was falling apart. I had been since the spring - when mom died. Our divorce was finalized in December and I hadn't had a single moment of internal peace for the majority of that year. Even at my wild, raucous Dirty 30 party, there wasn't enough vodka to make the pain and the guilt and the emptiness dissipate. Now, years later, it's still woven into my cells as if I had been born with the pain chromosome. Brown eyes, scoliosis, and grief.

However, dear reader, this isn't a sad story. This is a wild, messed-up, raunchy tell-all of my adventures in life after death, divorce, and 30. My name is Joelys Jeffries, but everyone calls me Joe. This is gonna get real personal, fast. Hang on.

## Chapter 1: Mama's Gotta Pay the Bills

I wasn't paying attention.

I wasn't distracted or on my phone. I wasn't eating or applying lipstick (as the cop so chauvinistically asked). I'm usually a very cautious driver, a granny my ex-husband used to say. To this day, I don't know how I could be so careless. I wasn't paying attention.

I was talking to my daughter. I was excited, happy for the first time in weeks. We'd just visited my father and we were headed to my best friend's house to drop off a big pot and my chili recipe for her company chili cook-off. I usually wouldn't let my daughter sit up front, but she had begged and I thought it wouldn't be so bad, just this one time. It was a rare sunny, clear day in Portland, OR, and these are not to be wasted. I hadn't told the kids yet, but I had budgeted for us to go to the zoo that afternoon. We hadn't had much fun since their dad moved out that rainy night in August. They deserved a break.

I loved my SUV. It wasn't new, but it was in great shape. My ex had found it in the Nickel ads and we paid cash. It had a killer sound system and more than enough space for a family. I got it in the divorce. I used to laugh when people asked me if I was concerned about roll-overs. The car was a tank, nothing bad could ever happen. I was wrong.

I saw the station wagon in my periphery. It was going to t-bone us, on the driver's side. My son was right behind me. It was coming too fast. I didn't have much time to react. Knowing my only option was to accelerate and hope to get past the other car, I gunned it. The wagon still made impact, hard, on our back corner. We started to spin.

The Bare Naked Ladies were taking One, One, One for their loneliness when I realized we were tipping over. Before they could finish the hook, we'd rolled three times landing on the driver's side. My daughter was dangling above me, screaming. I couldn't see my son. I yelled back to him and he replied with a shaky, "I'm ok." I was trapped, almost upside down and could barely move. I used my free hand to find and hold my daughter's.

It was a blur after that. I remember some guy, I have no idea who, hulked out on my back hatch and my son was able to climb out with ease. I remember the firemen giving me options, after they cut my daughter free from her seatbelt and she walked out of the hole where our front windshield used to be. I could do some gymnastics to exit the same way or wait for them to cut the roof off my car. They helped push my trapped leg to freedom and walk to the waiting ambulance. My shoulder was killing me and I could barely move my arm. My jaw hurt, I think it collided with my daughter's head.

We didn't need an ambulance, but I didn't argue. My daughter had a nasty, little cut on her leg and I wanted everyone examined just in case. The EMT tried to lay me in a bed, but I told him I was fine to sit with my children. He was taking my blood pressure and I started laughing. Loud, echoing laughter, contagious to my children and unsupressable. Tears formed in my eyes and I couldn't breathe. My daughter, Nat, caught her air enough to ask why were laughing.

"My mother always told me to wear clean underwear in case I was ever in an accident!" I coughed out.

"Well," She giggled. "Are you?"

"I'm not wearing any!" I exclaim and everyone, my son and the EMTs included, burst into laughter.

Later, in the emergency room, getting everyone checked out, the sexist cop would explain that the other car had sent us into a spin, causing the tire to separate from the wheel. The bare wheel dug into the asphalt of the road and sent the SUV into the roll-over. He would also inform me that every witness saw the same thing: I blew through the red light.

It was my fault.

I endangered my children's lives with my carelessness. I had lost focus at exactly the wrong moment and I had 3 stitches on my daughter's knee, a dislocated shoulder, and a fat ticket to prove it.

\*\*\*

My SUV was totaled. I was fortunate to have my old Toyota Camry, in terrible shape but drivable. Because I was at fault, my insurance wasn't going to replace our family car. I wondered what else life could throw at me.

***

Paying my ticket wasn't part of my already tight budget. I asked the power company for an extension and sold a diamond necklace of my mother's. It wasn't my style and I was only holding onto it in case my daughter wanted it someday. I don't buy diamonds, for ethical reasons. My own engagement ring was a department store rhinestone.

Divorce brought almost instant poverty for my children and myself. I received roughly a thousand dollars a month in financial aid/loans for going to school. That money combined with my child support was more than enough to pay for a simplified version of my life. We tightened our belts (well, metaphorically, I did NOT benefit from the divorce diet) and survived. It was hard, but we managed. I was grateful my children aren't materialistic. I felt terrible every time I had to say no, especially to little treats they had been accustomed to when we lived on their father's income.

Want to feel like a complete loser? Explain to a seven your old that his $4.99 pack of Pokemon cards isn't affordable right now.

***

I was surprised when I got the ambulance bill. After two hours of phone calls, I learned that neither my car nor health insurance were going to cover it. $840 for a four mile ride to the hospital and a blood pressure test. Tears in my eyes, I called the ambulance company to ask about a payment plan.

\*\*\*

My second quarter at the school, despite earning excellent grades, the financial aid paperwork was somehow screwed up and I did not get the fat check I was expecting. My savings had been wiped out paying off the small amount of debt James and I split in the divorce. My mortgage payment was due in 10 days and I had no intention of falling behind.

I assessed my options. No loans available, even from friends or family - all struggling as much as I was. I could tap into my equity on my home, but it would take too much time and raise my payment. I had a credit card for emergencies, but I'd already put the water heater on it and wouldn't have a high enough credit limit. Even the vulturous pay-day loan was off the table - I don't have a job. And if I took whatever job would take me, right away, I wouldn't see a paycheck in time, nor would it be enough. I had nothing of value to sell, other than my beat-up, 250K+ mile Toyota, but what would we do without a vehicle? For a brief moment, I considered giving up. Hopeless isn't a good look for me. Somehow - and to this day I have literally no idea where I found the chutzpah - I came up with a plan.

I purchased a gently-used massage table and rented a cheap room. I carefully worded an ad on craigslist offering 'release massage', claiming it was guaranteed to 'leave you happy'. To the reader lost in the terminology: I was offering to rub men's bodies and jack them off. I paused at my laptop as I tried to decide on a price. The pause wasn't hesitation, I'd already invested in the room and the table. I was in. How much value do I assign on my dignity? How do I balance the market for such things, stay competitive, but also not insult myself?

I decided on $90. The last massage I had received was $60 (back when I had the luxury of my husband's income) and I figured thirty was fair for the extra service. Also, at $90 it would weed out the undesirables, I'd hoped, while still being one of the more affordable of the other listings I researched. Ten minutes after my ad went live I had 20 replies. I didn't reply to the ones with poor grammar or obvious bots. Within the hour, I had five clients booked for the night. My heart racing with fear and anxiety and a little excitement, I opened up shop for my first client.

He was a short, slight man with auburn hair. His name was Adam and I laughed to myself at his being the first man on my table. I faked bravado and acted as if I'd done this a hundred times. At this point you might be wondering a few things: why did I pick massage and not just prostitution? How did I think I could pass myself off as a massage therapist? What on earth was I thinking?! I don't have answers to the latter other than I was desperate and maybe not thinking much at all. I picked massage because I had gone to school for it when I was 18. I quit when I got pregnant with my oldest, but I was almost done. I knew the basics, certainly, even after all these years. We'd discussed the dangers of 'release massage' in school and I guess that left a seed of an idea in my crazy, broken mind. It certainly seemed safer than selling my whole body.

Adam was nervous. I tried to put him at ease but my own nerves were betraying me. I knocked over my bottle of massage oil and slipped in the puddle. Adam quickly learned that I am clumsy and that I rarely wear underwear. We laughed and it helped. He disrobed and I got to work. My training had been years before but I was somewhat practiced, giving James frequent rubs. Adam's moans and growls told me I still had talent. I watched the clock and I worked his muscles and had him flip over. I carefully draped the towel as I had been trained and realized it wasn't necessary. I kept the towel in place though, still not 100% certain I would be able to go through with my big plan. I rubbed his shoulders, using a Thai technique I barely remembered. I thought of the caricature of a Chinese woman that had been one of the teachers at massage school. She was 4ft tall and 100 years old and stronger than any of us. We'd made fun of her, lovingly. Would she be disappointed in me? Proud of my ingenuity? I worked Adam's chest and neck, fighting a shake in my hands.

I'm not a prude, certainly. Before I was married I had about 15 partners. I was fast and easy as a teen and young adult. I liked sex and never viewed it as shameful or something to be preserved from or awarded to men. I'd always dressed provocatively. I like my curves and shorter dresses look best on me. Dealing with shorter dresses and my intense dislike of undergarments sucks, but pants suck more. I like showing cleavage; I've got great tits. I'm also partially Puerto Rican and look best in bright colors. My best friend once said I've got the style of sexy kindergarten teacher.

This wasn't my first time seeing a man naked after

divorce. I had a fling way too soon into singledom. A friend that had been sniffing around for awhile, Kyle. He's a weird guy, a metalhead with a crappy job and a crappier attitude. We had lackluster sex a few times and parted ways.

I moved to Adam's thighs. He was already hard, clearly evident under the cheap motel towel. I slid it up and had a new fear: what if I couldn't finish the job? Not because of nerves, but lack of skill? Some men are hard to get off. Would I offer a refund? How long should I try? I had 30 minutes until the next appointment. I took a deep breath and readied myself. I squirted the oil on his engorged and, to be honest, nicely-sized dick and wrapped my hand around it with the bravado of porn star.

A minute later I was aiming his spunk toward the towel. I wiped my hands on the same towel and folded it in half for him. I washed my hands while he started to get dressed. I made a mental note to call front desk and ask for more towels. I realized, then, I was a complete idiot. I hadn't asked for payment first. He could walk right out of here and I could do nothing about it. I felt vulnerable and sick until he reached for his wallet and handed me a hundred dollar bill. I asked if he wanted change and he smiled and said it was a tip. He exited quickly and I sat, examining the money. Ben Franklin smirked at me in what I assigned as approval. It wasn't exactly the easiest hundred bucks I'd ever earned, but it sure beat minimum wage.

The rest of that night was a blur. Four of the five appointments showed and I made $420 in 'donations' and tips. It was around midnight and I was exhausted.

I lamented at the awful motel mattress and considered driving home for sleep, but I had two more appointments set for the morning.

\*\*\*

Waking from a strange dream on that shitty bed, I sat up and assessed how I felt about what I had done the night before. I don't hold much faith in dream analysis but clearly my brain wanted me to at least think about my actions.

In the dream, my mother was chastising me for my messy room. She was angrily picking up my clothes and throwing them at me. The longer this went on, the louder and more out-of-control she became. One of my shoes was thrown, hard, against my vanity and shattered the mirror. I stared at my fractured reflection, unable to recognize my own face.

I decided to believe this was just chemicals washing over my brain and not to read a thing into it.

\*\*\*

I had the whole weekend to myself. The kids were with their dad until Sunday at 3pm. My goal was to earn enough for my $900 mortgage, plus the cost of the table and two nights at the motel. I'd reached my goal Saturday afternoon. I was fatigued; my body wasn't used to hours of standing and manual labor. Counting the money became my mantra. Between clients, I would hold it and flip thru the bills. When I reached $1200 I still had dozens of unanswered replies to my ad. I weighed my options. Calling this a one time thing and find a real job was considered and dismissed. I had tried to get work. I was rejected by fast food restaurants because of my scheduling needs. I also considered calling it good and relaxing the rest of the weekend. I flipped through the cash again. I thought about taking my kids to their favorite diner. We used to go once or twice a month. The place had huge, fluffy pancakes and sassy waitresses. I hadn't taken them there once since the divorce. I thought about the squeak in the breaks on the Toyota. I thought about the fancy salon conditioner I used to buy. Reality set in when I remembered the ambulance bill and the fact that my daughter needed new sneakers. The breaking point was actually when I remembered the water bill was overdue and I needed another $120.

I set more appointments.

By noon on Sunday, I checked out of the motel with $2,440. My arms ached and my head was spinning. I'd barely slept the night before, working until 2am and waking in time for a man that wanted a massage at 6am. He was using his normal gym time as his cover. He told me I could skip the massage and he'd give me $200 if I used my mouth instead. My reservations toward such things had vacated 7 or 8 dicks before. My arms and wrists grateful for the break, I blew him on the edge of the shitty bed. Instead of shame or disapproval, all I felt was relief. Two hundred dollars for less than ten minutes of work. That's $20/minute, more than doctors and lawyers make.

Sitting in my car, I grabbed my notepad from school out of my backpack. I budgeted out all my hard-earned cash, making sure bills were paid and throwing a couple hundred into savings. After double checking my math, I realized I'd still have over a couple hundred bucks to blow, if I wanted. I drove to a coffee stand, treating myself to a delicious white chocolate mocha. I couldn't remember the last time I'd enjoyed such a simple treat. I had certainly earned this one. I ordered it with an extra shot to combat the lethargy and tipped generously. I parked nearby and assessed the situation. I had about two and half hours to kill before I needed to pick up my kids. I sipped my mocha and reflected on the events of the last two days and nights.

Most of the men were surprisingly good-looking. I felt more wedding rings than bare fingers. My face started to tense up with emotion when I made that realization, but I reminded myself that I no longer valued marriage. The institution had lost my respect the day James called me worthless because I couldn't keep the house clean enough. In hindsight, I should have called an attorney then: I fell out of love with him in that very moment. We lasted almost another year after that fight. To be fair, he apologized and I was a terrible housekeeper. It was always a flawed pairing. He thought I was weird and reckless. He was charmed by my unique ways in the beginning, but spent years trying to squeeze me into a mold in which I would never fit.

I reallocated my feelings of regret over my deeds of this weekend. I refuse to accept guilt for others' infidelity. I provided a service, a clearly wanted one, and I am not culpable for their actions.

Most of the men were rather polite and respectful. A few were curt, or pushy. I didn't like the pushy.

Pushing me to offer more, to get undressed, to let them touch me, to fuck me. I hated it. I built this boundary, as arbitrary as it may seem, and they had no respect for it. Or me.

But, back to the two Benjamins burning a hole in my wallet. I finished my coffee and started my car. I drove straight to the beauty supply store and got a big bottle of my coveted Redkin detangling conditioner and sprang for a new bottle of Morrocan Oil too. I felt a twinge of guilt as I handed the cashier the money, the same way I always felt whenever I spent money on myself. I shrugged it off and even chuckled when I reminded myself how hard I'd worked for this. I love my hair; it's the only thing I'm vain about. I spent hours every month dying it gorgeous but shockingly bright colors: pinks and blues and fire engine red. It was daring but lovely. It was also incredibly damaging and required TLC.

Exhaustion overwhelmed me suddenly, so I set an alarm on my phone and napped in my car, right there in the parking lot. I woke refreshed and excited to treat the kids. They climbed into the car grumpy but that soon switched to my contagious excitement. They knew something was off when I didn't take the normal exit to our house. Questions were flying but I only gave them vague, mom-like answers, "You'll see when we get there!" It reminded me of our old life, being able to treat them to 'just because' adventures and surprises. For the first time in awhile, despite how I'd spent my weekend, I felt normal. Perhaps, this is how my new version of happy feels.

**Chapter 2: Love Ain't Easy**

Divorce left me bitter toward commitment. My new job affirmed the theory. Men cheat. The nicest family-man will get a handy with his massage and go home to his lovely wife. I witnessed it repeatedly, so often I started to think it better than typical cheating. No emotions, no victims. Simply needs met without strings. I also started to wonder what was wrong with American wives. Every man who opened up about it had the same story, "She never touches me anymore. We have sex maybe once a month."

Meanwhile, I was having crazy good sex. The job lowered my inhibitions. I attacked single life with the vim and vigor of a college freshman raised by a helicopter mom. Finally free, I experimented with casual sex and one night stands. I had some fun, but mostly it left me feeling empty. I think sex is better when you have a connection.

And then I met Henry. We were at a party thrown by an old friend in South Portland. Hank, as I would later call him under extreme protest, was wealthy and remarkably successful. Despite being a decade and a half older than me, he was also rather handsome. I cited an article he'd written for a wildly pretentious publication, surprising him. My then hot pink hair and libidinous way of dressing often gave people the wrong impression of me. We exchanged witty banter way above my societal caste and then I blew him in my friend's retro-mod guest bathroom. Hank was brilliant and passionate and made me feel special.

Hank was also, regrettably, married.

We kept our relations textual for a couple months after the party. Flirting via iPhone was safe. It wasn't crossing my boundaries. He suggested meetups and weekend trips, but I never took the bait — until he offered PenCon. He told me he was lecturing at America's largest conference devoted to writing utensils and I was drooled at the possibility of attending. It was in Ohio, practically another world as far as I was concerned. He offered me free airfare, convention entrance, Cleveland's finest restaurants, and half of his bed. The only vacation I had taken in the last decade was to the Oregon Coast. On my honeymoon. I arranged childcare and agreed to join him.

My fascination with pens started early. I noticed how the heavy, thick pens from the bank wrote smoother and more consistently than the crystalline Bics my mother always bought me. I asked for a fountain pen that next Christmas. I spent hours with practice books from the library and perfected my italic calligraphy by age nine. I worked on other forms of lettering and script, mastering each within weeks. By middle school, I was the go-to girl for any sign or banner that needed fabrication. In high school, I applied for an internship at a sign shop. I was elated at the idea of helping to make real signs for banks and shops and festivals. At the interview I was told the position always went to boys because they needed the muscle. Devastation beat outrage and I silently accepted the unfair rejection.

In hindsight, it was that rejection that paved the road I ended up taking. My parents didn't encourage me to look into college. We had no money for it. I was smart but my grades weren't good enough for scholarships.

I was too boy-crazy to ever care about my future. There's an immediacy that poverty breeds into you. You have to act fast, now. You never know what tomorrow brings so you look for temporary fixes instead of long-term solutions. Losing that internship, the only time I'd made an effort toward my own future, was crushing to me.

It was an internship that served as the cover story for Hank and me. I was his sassy, colorful intern and had to behave as such in public. He only held my hand on the plane after double checking every face he could see for familiarity. Once he felt we were clear, he whispered filthy words into my ear as we took off, describing exactly what he was going to do to me when we were in the safety of his room.

We arrived in time for the meet-and-greet cocktail hour being thrown in his honor. I stayed in the background, watching his laptop bag and making sure my legs were properly crossed. A middle-aged, razor thin professional woman took the seat next me. She shot me a knowing look and asked, "Assistant or mistress?"

"Intern." I threw back with feigned contempt.

"Sure." She said with another know-it-all look and a wink.

Her skinny ass recieved my best trailer-park stare down and she darted out of her chair. I may look and dress like a slutty Miss. Frizzle but I am 50% white trash and 50% Puerto Rican and 100% not about to be judged by anyone. Hank gave a me a concerned look and I reassured him with a nonchalant shrug. I surveyed the room for any other subtle criticism. I seemed to be mostly ignored. Except by the champaign waiter, who was staring at my cleavage. He was rewarded a better angle while I pretended to adjust my dress.

When Hank could gracefully exit, he led me to his room and wrecked my body until I begged him for respite. We slept in an adorable half cuddle for awhile until his hands found my hips again. He was in me before I was fully awake. His thick member filled me in ways I hadn't felt in ages. I was already sore but I didn't ask him to stop. I could feel his carnal want on every inch of my skin. When I suggested a break for lube he roughly pushed my legs up and licked me until I screamed. He was fucking me again before I caught my air. His lips caught mine while he came deeply inside me. It was only then he remembered to ask about birth control.

"It's all good." I said lightly, slightly upset by the abruptness of his tone.

Impatiently, he asked, "Good how? Joe, what do you use?"

"Tubal ligation." I was short and snotty because I desperately did not want to tell him how safe we were from some unwanted love child. A complication from the c-section with my son had left me with about half of my former female anatomy. A complication from which took me years to fully recover. A complication that left me bitter, angry. Not that I want any more kids; oh, hell no. I hate that I don't have the option and James does. If he so desires, we could just be his starter family. Practice wife and brats to be discarded for a better model with superior genes. The thought filled me with rage. I asked a lawyer friend if I could demand a vasectomy in a divorce petition.

Hank paused as if debating how to proceed. He was incredibly conscientious with his words, always. He'd call a surprising or eventful action 'wild' instead of 'crazy' in effort to destigmatize mental illness. He was also born in Canada and had a crisp, thoughtful accent. After deciding, he said evenly, "You're a bit young for that."

It was then I remembered that I had fibbed on my age a bit. Making myself 27 instead of 31. I don't know why other than vanity.

"Well, I had a boy and a girl and that's all you need." I laughed for good measure, hoping we were done with the questioning. We never discuss my kids or his family. These things were off-limits. He seemed to accept my answer as his kisses trailed down my neck.

\*\*\*

I broke away from my 'intern' duties during the convention on the second full day, rather than listen to his lecture again. I checked out the promotional booths. I scored some swag for the kids and purchased a couple new fountain pens for myself. The famous Bic logo, huge, at least six feet wide, caught my eye. I thought back to the tiny bed James and I shared in our first apartment. I was pregnant and we were to wed the next day. We were discussing honeymoon options and I said I wanted to tour the Bic Pen factory in Connecticut. He laughed heartily and called me a weirdo. We stayed at his mother's timeshare on the coast.

I wasn't a weirdo here.

\*\*\*

Three days whirled by with fine dinners, interesting lectures, role playing an intern, and so much sex. I had to stop at a pharmacy for something to quiet the friction burns inside me. Hank educated me in the etiquette of dim sum and I introduced him to Neutral Milk Hotel. I noticed on day two he would call me Love when we were free and clear. "Would you like a coffee, Love?" It thrilled and terrified me, like all great adventures.

On our final night, I stared at his profile back-lit from the light we'd left on in the bathroom. I wanted to trace the curve of his Roman nose and memorize every beard hair. I loved the way he always touched his beard when he was trying to remember something. I loved the way he looked at me, as if I was the most desirable being on Earth. I loved his smell. Snapping into reality I reminded myself that none of this, not one moment, was rightfully mine.

**Chapter 3: Borrowed and Blue**

We'd always have Ohio. And Chicago. And Vegas and LA. Hank and I had many adventures throughout that year. He'd also get us suites nearby when we could both spare a weekend.

Our relationship cut into my work, but a kind neighbor lady started watching the kids one night a week so I could book clients. Even after my financial aid was reinstated I kept massaging. I liked the easy money. I liked saying yes when my kids asked for non-necessities. Plus, in all honesty, I got a perverse pleasure in the work. It was dirty-hot, sinful. I dyed my hair jet black with lavender tips to mark my new badassness. I was juggling it all: classes, massages, momming, staying active in the PTO, and an affair.

That fall brought my best friend's wedding. Massive amounts of tension plagued me as it grew closer. Kennedy became my instant and forever best friend in a bathroom in 9th grade. She found me crying in a stall and asked if I was alright. A boy that I had a huge crush on had made fun of my visible panty line in front of our whole English class. Everyone started calling me 'granny-panties' in a chant. I made two major changes that day: I stopped wearing underwear and K (as I call her, she calls me J) became my closest friend. She asked me to be maid-of-honor right after Derek French proposed, two years ago. I readily accepted, not counting on one, tiny event:

My own dissolution of marriage, and subsequent revulsion to weddings.

Rather than being an adult and telling her my reservations and feelings, I was a 12-year-old and picked a fight. I picked one big enough to get her too angry to have me in the bridal party but not forever friendship ending. I called her horrible, untrue things and I regret that every day. We never fully healed. A couple months before the big day, we made up and I scored an invite. I turned down an invitation to go to Hong Kong with Hank and asked if I could still give a speech. It was a lovely wedding and I cried like I was the one giving away the bride. In some ways, I was.

In our 20s, she was the single one with wild adventures and I was the married one with stability. Once again, we weren't on the same level. Kennedy and I had swapped roles, but it's different in your 30s. She was just selective, cautious; I was unwanted, discarded. I wished her well, of course, but it was also the mark of a major change in our friendship. Already, I was keeping things from her. Not just my motives for the fight. I kept my new business venture a secret, knowing she wouldn't approve and worry for my safety. My relationship with Hank, a newly blessed bride would not approve of the choices I was making! Even the strongest windshield will break if chips aren't correctly repaired.

\*\*\*

James wanted a sit-down meeting to discuss my new travel schedule.

He told me he'd noticed that the kids mentioned more time with sitters and their grandfather. He was curious why I was spending so much time away from home. I told him, nicely, it was none of his business, but went with the internship story.

"Aren't you a little old to be an intern?" He quipped.

"Sorry, the years I *should* have spent on education and career development were *actually* spent on raising your babies and cooking your dinners."

He apologized for his snottiness. I apologized for mine. We worked out the parenting schedule for the upcoming few months. We also agreed that if I had more travel in the future, I would ask him if he could take the kids before I arranged a sitter.

***

When Hank returned from Hong Kong, he booked us our favorite suite. It had this large, beige soaking tub that was supposed to be in the shape of a heart. All I saw was a giant ball-sack which amused me endlessly. He brought Settlers of Catan and I brought high quality hard cider. It wasn't just a bang-fest. We talked and laughed and enjoyed each other's company. I didn't need vaginal numbing cream. As we wore off our energy, we climbed into the tub and relaxed, sharing a comfortable silence. Once again, I studied his handsome profile. Maybe it was leftover edification I reached at Kennedy's wedding or maybe I'd just sensed what was to come, but in that moment I acknowledged two things. First, I was in love with Hank. But also, he wasn't mine to love. He was borrowed.

After our bath, we made love. We shared our bodies in a tender, soft way we'd never tried before. As hokey as it sounds, we expressed our feelings without a word. It was quiet, almost reverent. We finished together and he held my whole body in his as we both shook. It was powerful and unforgettable.

He gently sat up and pulled a blanket over us. I could tell he was searching for the right words, in that way he always does. I was hopeful and yet feared what he had to say.

"Joe," He started with a slight creak to his usual even tone, "I'm taking the CEO position I was offered."

I vaguely remembered this. He mentioned it passing, but it seemed at the time he wasn't interested at all. It would mean a move for his family. In hindsight, I may have stopped listening when he mentioned them. They needed to stay foreign to me for my mental survival. I didn't know what to say other than, "Yeah?"

"Yeah." He sighed with weight. I looked up at him, he appeared nervous. Was he ending it? I waited, anxious and maybe relieved.

"I've started looking at apartments. But that was silly because I don't know if you'd say yes or maybe you'd want a house." He half chuckled, shakily.

"If I'd want...wait, say yes to what?" I asked, completely lost.

"My wife refuses to move. I understand, our kids have roots and friends. Moving them now would be cruel." He paused. I waited, dumbfounded. "I'd have to go back every other weekend, sometimes more. But I'd be all yours during the week."

What he wanted was starting to click. Incapable of speech, I motioned with my hand for him continue.

"Joelys Jeffries, I love you and want to be with you. I want you to move to Los Angeles with me. I would get you a house or," he laughed again, "or an apartment or a cabin or whatever you want to live in. We could be together most of the time. I would take care of you and your kids, financially. This position is very lucrative. You wouldn't want for anything."

"You want...." the words were not coming together for me. "You want me to move? And live with you?"

"Well," He started quickly, "I would have to keep a little apartment for appearance sake, of course. But I would spend most of my time with you at your place. I mean, of course, not at first. We'd let your kids get to know me. We can tell them whatever you want. I can get you a job with the company, you're smart as a whip and -"

"Hank!" I cut off his babbling. "Slow down, please. I'm processing what you're asking of me."

"Sorry, Love. I'm excited."

"So, you'd stay married?" I asked.

"Yes."

"And you'd come home to your *wife* on weekends?" I asked pointedly.

"No, not every weekend. Maybe a few weeks in the summer. Not for her, Love. For the kids." He was flustered. This wasn't going to his plan. "Can't you see, this way we can be together and not hurt anyone."

"You think no one would get hurt in that scenario?" My voice was tight, sharp. I was fighting the urge to cry.

"Love, Joe, please be logical. I have no prenup. If I divorced, she'd get almost everything. My children would hate me. My life would be over. If you move with me, we could have it all. You could finish your degree or work, whatever you want. I don't love her, I love -"

"Stop." I cut him short again. I was afraid if I heard him say it one more time, I would break apart. My voice filled with emotion, I continued, "What about MY children?"

"I told you, Love. I would take care of you all. I'm sure they'd like me. They'd love LA; there's so much to do." He was pleading now.

"Why would I move my children? They have roots too. Why would I move them so far from their father?" I was more even now, calmer.

"They have a father? I just assumed..." His voice trailed off. "Were you married to him?"

"Yes, of course I was. I got divorced last year. Where do you think they go during our weekend getaways?" At this moment Hank realized how little he actually knew about me. I could see it in his face. He looked betrayed. I went further, "Oh, and I'm actually 31." He looked stunned. We sat in silence for a few beats, and it was no longer comfortable.

"I don't understand why you didn't mention your divorce to me." He was hiding his anger in that polite, Canadian way.

"So you, what, assumed I was just a single mom? No baby-daddies? Too slutty to know who the father was?" I didn't have much room to be critical here. I was being snarky anyway.

"Joelys, in a thousand years I could never understand how a man would divorce you or let you go. I figured you wanted to be on your own. You're so self-confident; you," He stopped briefly, "you're amazing."

My eyes welled in tears. No matter what happens, I knew in that moment Hank touched something deeply broken in me. I clung to him, quietly crying into his lap.

"The age thing doesn't matter either. I'm still way too old for you." He laughed lightly. We didn't joke about the age difference ever. Especially after that time the waitress asked if he was enjoying a night out with his daughter. I took a deep breath.

"Hank, I love you but I cannot move to LA. I can...not contin-" I gasped for air, "continue...this aff-"

"I know, Love. Quiet now." He stroked my hair and let my answer linger in the unsaid but known.

He kept stroking my hair until I fell asleep. In the morning, I woke alone.

I packed quickly and said a silent farewell to the ballsack tub, to our love, and to the potential of what we could have had.

**Chapter 4: Rebounds Only Make Sense in Sports**

Once again, I had to hide my emotional pain from my children. When my daughter caught me crying at the sink, she hugged me tight. Assuming it was about her father, she told me she didn't have to spend

Thanksgiving with him. It was an easy guess for her 11-year-old mind, as we'd just talked about it.

I'd never liked the holiday. It was easy for me to give it to James. He has the big, close family that all gather annually at his Aunt's house and share dry turkey and prayer. I prefer food with flavor and don't believe in any Gods. My family always did enchiladas and horror movies. I'd miss my kids but I was looking forward to a return to my roots.

I hugged her tight and expressed how happy it made me that she gets to go with her dad and share the holiday with his family.

"Then why were you crying?" She asked.

I couldn't begin to tell her the truth. I missed Hank. But, also, I was mourning the life I'd turned down. An easy, cared-for life in sunny Los Angeles - with its events, arts, and cultural diversity. I loved the Pacific Northwest, but damn, it's fucking white here. Even my children had their father's aryan genes, blondes with blue eyes. I was often asked if I was the nanny.

"Sometimes, my darling, you can be both happy and sad. I am happy that you get a fun Thanksgiving; I'm sad that I don't get to be a part of it. And that's ok. It's ok to feel sad at sad things. Here's the deal: I love YOU and your happiness is way more important than my own." She seemed pleased with that answer and asked for a cheese stick.

I continued washing the dishes and ruminated on James and his family. After ten years together, we created a shared life. We bought a house that is now only my own. We trained a dog that now only lives with him. We fell in love with each other's families. He adores my father as his own and from him, I found the big, nosy extended family I'd always wanted.

But I didn't get to keep his family. It was a week after the split that I noticed my facebook friends/family list was a little lighter. That hurt. I tried to make plans with his father when he visited and it was made clear that he'd only like to see the kids. That hurt too. And a few months later, his mom's annual Christmas Newsletter arrived. A paragraph to each son and family. I was not mentioned.

Of course I wasn't. That would be weird, right? I'm not in the family anymore. I was just the incubator of the grandkids.

Ok, maybe that was harsh.

A few weeks ago, I picked up the monkeys after their dad-weekend. Almost as an afterthought, ex-hubby mentioned his Aunt's passing. His aunt was 190 and this wasn't a huge surprise. But, it caught me off-guard. I started crying. Hard. She's gone. She was like a second mom to him. She was such a big, strong woman. She hated me, and I never cared because I respected her so much. And she's gone.

I was not invited to mourn with the family. Just like when his grandmother passed last winter. My children had to go to their first traditional, Christian funeral without me.

I am no longer welcome in the family that I wanted, that I worked so hard to be accepted by, that I loved and cherished. I can joke about the dry turkey, but I would miss it. With them I finally felt at home, like I belonged somewhere, a glimpse into a functional family not centered on liquor and partying. Now I'm in the cold shadow of once knowing that love and losing it.

That's the worst part of divorce. For me, anyway. C'est la vie, I'll always have enchiladas.

\*\*\*

They left the day before Thanksgiving to avoid traffic. That night, silent in the usually obnoxious, loud house, I felt profoundly alone. I thought about trying to book some massages, but I didn't want to drive anywhere. Or work, really. I logged onto craigslist while I debated my options I got another one of my fantastic ideas. I would place an ad looking for company.

*"I'm alone this Thanksgiving and don't want to be. Maybe you are too. Maybe you're not able to see your family or don't want to. Here's what I propose: Let's not be alone. SHF seeks SM for one night (and ONLY one night) of togetherness. Not just sex, an affectionate night where we talk and cuddle and eat and watch movies. Please be witty and tall."*

I read each reply as they poured into my inbox. As was my habit, I instantly deleted any with dick pics or really bad grammar. A lot of them read like a cut and paste reply they give to every ad placed. I ignored those too. I was interested in one reply from a handsome, well-spoken man until I realized he was the husband of one of the moms I knew from my son's school. I was mentally shaming him when Scott's email came in. The words and tone seemed so genuine. He was the only applicant I replied to.

We spent the holiday together and discovered we had amazing chemistry. He was stupid tall, 6'4", and rail thin. His long, slender fingers grabbed me with authority, as if he'd owned me his whole life. The sex was passionate and giving; he took the time to explore my every curve. We discovered a mutual obsession with his tongue on my pussy. I had never met a man hungrier for me. We also talked and got to know each other. Although I could tell we couldn't be more different, ideologically, I was fascinated with his every word.

Scott called me his girlfriend a couple weeks later. I didn't correct him. He told me he loved me on Christmas day. I introduced him to my children later that night. We were talking about living together by New Year's.

His hyper energy was contagious. Just being near him was better than coffee. It wasn't just the way he'd throw my dress up and lick me, often, anywhere. It was everything about him. Quick minded, quick temper, passionate speech, and a ridiculously fast car. He was cocaine, in human form. Cocaine that could make me climax in under a minute. I was hooked.

The addiction and the mania blinded me to his less than stellar qualities. That quick temper stung me a few times. He seemingly always had a beer in his hand, and he wasn't always a fun drinker. He'd get loud and super racist. He wasn't educated but thought he was an expert in most everything. He was possessive and controlling over my time and attention. Kennedy hated him. I didn't put much stock in her opinion, though; she always hated my boyfriends. Scott and I fought a lot. We settled most spats and disagreements the same way - the perpetual stubble of his face rubbing against my thick thighs. On some level I knew how unhealthy we were, but I didn't care.

It wasn't just the constant and satisfying cunnilingous. I mean, come on, that helped. But, I loved his mania. I loved his unapologetic and unbreakable love for me. I loved his giving spirit. I love the fire we had when it got political and he'd throw me down on the couch and call me the liberal devil woman. I loved how my Puerto Rican ass felt somehow smaller in his hands. I loved when he'd pull scary stunts in his Corvette. We had it up to 140 mph on the highway once. I loved how he'd grab me and make out with me randomly, as if he'd forgotten how it felt. I loved that he was free to be mine, just mine.

There was one small caveat to our love: he didn't know the truth about my side gig.

At first, I didn't tell him because it was certainly none of his business. I still had yet to tell my closest friends. And then, as it became clear that he would not approve, I decided not to tell him. It wasn't cheating, I justified. It's just a job. As far as he knew, I was a massage professional who provided outcall massage. He would even joke about happy endings sometimes and I would act offended. We were happy, why mess it up? I mentally decided to let my future self deal with it and quit when or if we got super serious.

By the end of January, he all but lived with me when he was in town. His work schedule was perfect for us. He would fly out to North Dakota for his job in the oil industry and work a couple weeks. The third week of the month, he'd fly to California to see his son. The fourth week of the month was all mine. We'd have all day to worship each other's bodies, shower, and pick the kids up from school. He'd take us all out for dinners and movies or bowling and sneak back into my room when they went to sleep. The kids adored him, especially my son. It was impossible to not like Scott - he was a cartoon character.

Our happiness lasted another couple months. When he was away, I could focus on my kids, my school, my home, my work. Our time together was a delicious bubble of orgasms and glee and fun. Occasionally, one of our problems would pop up, but it was so easy to dismiss when I had such limited time to enjoy him.

It was a frantic Sunday that we had made worse by just *one more* fuck. We had to get him to the airport and I needed a shower. He readied himself while I washed up. I pulled him into the water with me, even though he was half dressed. He was angry but easily calmed by my deep kisses, at least momentarily. He told me to focus and asked to use my laptop to double check his flight information. I let him go with a nod and a quick cheek kiss. I wasn't going to push him too far.

My laptop was perched weirdly on his endless lap when I walked in with my towel barely covering me. I gave him a quick flash and a wink. His expression didn't change. I asked if everything was alright.

"What the fuck is this shit, Joelys?" Whoa, full name. He never used my full name. What did he see on my laptop? I froze.

"You DO give happy endings?! You're a fucking whore?! How could you lie to me like this?!" He stood, livid, my laptop crashing to the floor. I was still frozen, naked and suddenly chilled to the bone. He roughly grabbed my shoulders and shook me. "Answer me, you fucking bitch!"

No words came but I tried to open my mouth. I'd never been handled like this. I'd never been caught in this big or kind of lie. Time seemed slower and I could feel my heartbeat all over my body. His strong arms spun me toward the bed and he screamed it again, inches from my face, "Answer me!!"

I wasn't breathing, but I tried opening my mouth again. That's when I saw his clenched hand wind back. I tried to dodge but it landed powerfully on my chest. My brain registered the pain as I started falling back, dropping my towel. I did not see his other fist coming. It hit my jaw so hard my neck cracked. I fell to the bed. Instinctively, my arms covered my face and I folded my body tightly into itself. I shook with terror as to what he'd do now. But I only heard him gasp and fall to the floor.

I focused on my breathing and assessed the situation. In breath. Out breath. He seemed to have stopped. I could hear him, it sounded like he was crying. In breath. Out breath. That did not mean I was safe. In breath. Where is my phone? Out breath. Who would I call? In. Out. Slower, Joey. Think. Grab your robe and book it outside. In. Out. He's faster than me. He's stronger than me. In. Out. I realized my head was pounding and my neck hurt. Everything hurt, but the pain was sharp in my neck. I peeked.

He was in a lump of his own on the floor, holding himself and bawling. It was quiet, but his shaking made it look violent. I shifted to a more comfortable position and pulled the blanket over myself. I found it in myself to speak: "Y-you need t-to leave." It was then I noticed how I was trembling with cold and the fear, and possibly adrenaline. He rose quickly and rushed to me talking fast.

"Baby, oh my God, baby! Are you ok? I can't believe I....baby, please, please know I would never... Are you ok? That wasn't me. I would NEVER....oh, god baby, what did I do? Can I sit here?" He was already sitting beside me. "Oh, God, do you need to see a doctor? Baby, please, you have to tell me if you're ok."

I had no idea what to do. He seemed safe, controlled, for the moment. But I could anger him again if I demand he leave. "I'm ok." That's the best I could do. He was crying again. He threw himself on me and sobbed into my chest. Involuntarily, I yelped in pain. He darted up. His face showed so much anguish, I knew his rage was over. I repeated, "I'm ok."

"Let me take you to the doctor. Your face is already swelling."

I found my ability to speak. "I can't go to a doctor. You'd go to jail. My ex could use this in court to take my kids. I think you should just go. You're going to miss your flight."

"Fuck my flight, Joe. I hit you. I'm a monster. I don't care if I go to jail."

"Can you get me some ice?" I had to get him away from me.

"Oh, of course." And he runs toward the kitchen. I carefully get up and grab my phone. My head was pounding now, making it hard to think. I had no idea who to call. My dad? My sick dad who can't walk a block without oxygen and shouldn't be driving? No. Kennedy? Oh, God no. She hates Scott and would insist I call the cops. I scrolled my contacts. I was trapped. I had isolated myself with my lies and bad choices, and I was stuck to deal with the consequences on my own. I made myself as comfortable as possible sitting on my bed and pulled the covers back up. I hid my phone under my leg.

He came in and I kept a calm look on my face. I put the ice on my jaw and asked him for some tylenol and vodka. In for a penny, in for a pound.

## Chapter 5: Carry On My Wayward Daughter

Why are commercial fabrics so damn ugly? Hunter green and maroon floral damask upholstered chairs lined the waiting room. I searched the room, again, for a familiar face. I'd prefer polite small talk to the terrible magazines offered. My butt is sweaty against the shitty fabric. I should have worn panties today. Dad's appointment should have been over a half hour ago. I let loose a loud sigh.

I hated being alone these days. My head was filled
with too many secrets, too much pain. Of course I had
to remind myself the last time I'd been at this hospital,
my mother died. The memory of her last breath, her
eyes searching for and landing on my father, it haunts
me. The greatest accomplishment in my mom's sad,
short life was her romance with the handsome and
charming Leeroy Jeffries. Yes, Leeroy. I told you I
was part white trash. I felt myself grow older, staring
at ugly chairs.

I didn't get the fabled 'great last moment' with my
mother. I didn't know she was dying until it was time
to pull her off the ventilator. I naively thought she
would get better. I knew she was sick, yes. I had no
idea what the drinking had done to her body until it
was too late. Her last words to me resonate to this
day. James and I were trying to comfort her as they
readied her throat for the ventilator. She pushed the
nurse away, and clearly, sternly said to us: "Would
you two just shut the fuck up!" I wouldn't trade that
moment for anything. It was true to her, to her nature.

My phone buzzed in my handbag. I didn't look. I knew
it was Scott. He always texts me on his break, around
this time. I'd rather see the chairs than read that text.

It wouldn't be mean, of course. Since the day he went
Mike Tyson on my chin, it'd been nothing but intense,
unending love and positivity. He stayed for three days
at my side, not letting me lift a finger. He replaced my
laptop with a much nicer model and apologized with
his every breath. Eventually, he had to get to work
and I got some air and some space. I told him I
needed to think about our situation and that I'd let him

know where we stood when he returned. I knew the *right* answer, obviously. I needed to dump his ass and never look back.

However, I did lie to him. I broke a very proud man's heart.

The door to the examination rooms opened and my pops sauntered out. Somehow, even wheeling an oxygen tank behind him, my father had bravado. I asked him what the doctor had said, annoyed I had to use him as a middle man. I should have been in there with him. Dad was too proud. A trend with the men in my life, I'm noticing.

"These idiots don't know shit." He wheezed, in a barking voice. Emphysema had changed his voice entirely. He made eye contact with the attractive nurse at the desk and with a wink, threw to her: "Except you, angel. You're aces."

I rolled my eyes and walked with him to the car. He complained about the garbage on the floorboards. I reminded him that I could always get him a bus pass. He turned his tank off and lit a cigarette. There was a time where I would have ripped it out of his mouth but I stopped trying. Let him kill himself, he's certainly not happy.

There was a time when I honestly believed my father was invincible. He could hot tar a roof all day, ride a motorcycle, play the guitar, and make anyone laugh. He was smart but approachable, capable but fun. He was good at everything. He had a perfect block capital handwriting, like an architect. I always pay attention to how people write. Scott also writes in perfect block capitals.

When I dropped my pops off, he asked if I needed gas money. Somethings never change.

\*\*\*

My precious white mocha had betrayed me, spilling all down my chest and on my dress, when the call came. The vice-principal at my daughter's school needed me to come right away. I didn't believe the words he'd said, something about her starting a fight. I knew it wasn't possible. My daughter, Nat (for Natalia), is incapable of violence. I mopped up the mess as best as I could and headed to her school.

Two surprises awaited me: a boy with an ice pack on his cheek and the fact that I knew the vice-principal. I knew him very well. He was one of my most regular clients. I hid a smile when I saw the color drain from his face. He offered me a seat next to a terrified-looking Nat. I took her hand and whispered in her ear: "I don't know what happened but I've got your back, mija. Always." She relaxed a little. I asked what happened.

"It seems," he started weirdly and cleared his throat, "It seems your daughter punched Jeremy Levold during lunch. There were many witnesses who say she punched him first and he did nothing physical toward her."

"I see." I wasn't sure what alternative universe I had stepped into. My daughter is the shyest, sweetest girl you could ever know. This was completely out of her character. "What happened Nat?" I asked simply.

"He called you a name."

"The boy did? Called ME a name? Why? Do we know him?"

"Mom, I'm so sorry." Nat started to cry. "I didn't want to hurt anyone. He wouldn't stop saying mean things."

"It's gonna be alright, sweetie." I tried to reassure her. I was dying of curiosity. What could this 6th grader have to say about me?

Mike, the vice-principal who happens to like butt-stuff, cleared his throat again. "It seems the boy, yes, was calling you something inappropriate."

"He's always making fun of me mom." Nat piped up. "The school never punishes him and gets worse and worse. I could take it until he call you a sl--" She couldn't finish.

"A s-l-u-t?" I spelled out. She nodded. I gave the perv in a cheap tie my best stare down.

After a few beats, he cleared his throat again and said, "Well, this is Nat's first offense and yes, Jeremy is known to tease kids so I think we can just give her a warning."

"I think that's fair." I maintained eye contact. "And what about the boy?"

"Oh, he'll be fine. The nurse said it's just a bruise."

"I'm glad to hear that. I meant what actions will be

taken against him?" I was like a pitbull with a steak now. Mr. ButtStuff was gonna lose an arm before I gave up. He hemmed and hawed a bit before agreeing that Jeremy violated the bullying and language rules and would have one afternoon detention. I called it a win and checked Nat out as excused. A girl's first punch deserves an ice cream.

I couldn't sleep that night. Had I sent her the wrong message? Violence is never the answer. Did she somehow know what had happened with Scott and think I was ok with punching? Would Principal McFingerInButt use this against me? It was my first time interacting with a client in the 'real world'. It was terrifying. Why would that asshole kid call me that? Was it the way I dressed? I finally put the day behind me, deciding to have a long talk with her about alternatives to hitting. Honestly, my gut reaction was spot-on. Good for her.

\*\*\*

Scott returned on a Friday. I did not pick him up from the airport and asked him to meet me at a bar downtown with cozy, private booths. I wanted public, but not too public. My bruises were healed but I was not. My heart still raced when I remembered how much fear and pain he caused.

The flowers in his hand were the eighth bouquet he'd given me since it happened. Since he hit me. I reinforced my will with an honest account of events. This man punched me twice. No amount of flowers, niceness, or apologies would change that.

He stoically accepted my decision to end our relationship. I encouraged him to seek some anger management or treatment and he said he'd already looked into it. I got emotional when I kissed his cheek as I left but did not look back. I then drove to cheap hotel and set up shop. Time for this slut to get some work done, the light bill won't pay itself.

## Chapter 6: With a Little Help From My Friends

Spring quarter at the community college brought a myriad of challenges to my life. Namely math 101. Even worse, I could only get the 8am class. Also my anthro prof was a weird man who seemed super interested in picking on me.

Socially, I had never been in a better place in my life. My experience with Scott made me realize I was isolated. In my married days, Kennedy was all the friendship I had time for. I had acquaintances, sure, but only one close friend. It was time to expand and find a larger pool of people to trust and confide in. First was Gene. Nerdy, funny, exceptionally brilliant and under-achieving Gene. We'd had one failed date but agreed instantly to be friends. I tried something with Gene that I had never done done before: total honesty. We were soon inseparable.

Gene's shitty car had just died and I had my old beater Toyota sitting around. Dad and I agreed that I could take over his Cadillac, since the doctors had taken away his license. I lent Gene my old car in exchange for a daily ride to school so I didn't have to deal with campus parking. The best part of my day was ofyen my ride with Gene. He'd honk, I'd jump into the car. We'd grab coffees at the Plaid Pantry and he'd smoke a bowl in the parking lot while we talked and laughed. Gene is probably the funniest man I'd ever known. He'd get me to the door of the maths building with 10 minutes to spare.

Kate would drop me off at home. She was so young when we met, I had trouble calling her a friend. I looked at it as more of a mentorship, originally. She was a running start student, attending college classes during her junior year in high school. Kate's social anxiety was palpable by anyone around. Skinny and fidgety, she was the kind of girl you just want to hug and make a cup of cocoa for. She also liked the crazy colored hair and we called ourselves The Skittles. She helped me to remember the advantages of age. She was also worshipped by my daughter.

I also had a new girl-gang I had latched onto. We had a secret handshake and everything. They were fun and got me out of the house. I started engaging with other students on campus. I got an asshole cat from the shelter. I don't like cats, but as a single woman - I was required by law to have one. I dated casually. I was definitely laughing more. Something else I had forgotten in my time being a wife/mommy-zombie: I can be really fun.

Waiting for Gene one morning, I dreaded going to anthro. The professor was getting weirder toward me. He'd ask me to answer very personal questions about my life in class. He had this annoyingly nasal voice that made me murderously angry. The day before in class he'd called me out for not wearing a bra. How was that even slightly appropriate?

Gene honked; I ran out, happy to see him. I asked him what he planned for the day.

"Get stoned, jack off, and sleep." Gene's life was pretty easy. I didn't envy his schedule (graveyard shift cooking at a truck stop), but I coveted his freedom.

"You don't work tonight, right?" I asked.

"Nope. Why?"

I had an idea. "Take me to math, wait around for the 50 minutes, and then I'll blow off the rest of my classes and we'll have an adventure. I just have to be back by 3:30."

"Avoiding creepy anthro guy?" He knew me oh, so well.

After math (you can't skip a single day in those kinds of classes - a lesson I learned my first quarter), I filled his, well my, gas tank and we decided to see what was two hours south of us. Of course, growing up in Portland/Vancouver I already knew. Gene was relatively new to the area, growing up in some podunk town in northern Washington State. I mentally reminded myself to email Prof WeirdoVonNeedsALife and off we went.

The drive allowed us time to talk. He told me about his frustrations with dating. He knew I was pretty adamant about staying single for the foreseeable future. The fiasco with Scott made me realize I wasn't in the place for a relationship. He helped me word the email explaining my absence. He suggested I use my dad's health but I like to avoid that kind of ju-ju. I went with migraine headache. That asshole prof gave attendance points but wouldn't count absences against you if you had a good excuse and emailed in advance.

We were in a heated debate over the subtle sexism of Star Trek when we rolled into Eugene, OR. Yes, the show had been groundbreaking in efforts to include women and people of color, and yes, there was a female captain; however, the short skirted uniform of Deanna Troi made her as much a prop as a character. We had no plan, just drive until something caught our eye. I saw a sign for a raptor center and started humming the Jurassic Park theme. We were there 10 minutes later.

Sadly, there were no dinosaurs. The center homed over 50 species of birds of prey. It was an excellent use of $8 admission ($5 for him, $3 for me with my student ID) of two hours of our time. We had perfect timing too: a parliament of owlets were hatched the week before and we got to stroke their fluffy, soft feathers. We also learned that baby owls are called owlets and a group of owls are called a parliament. Never stop learning, kids.

Sitting on a bench in the turkey vulture hut, I watched what must have been the ugliest bird I've ever seen pick at the bark of a tree. According to the signs, her name was Kali and she was abandoned as an egg. My mama hormones kicked in and I instantly loved her. I watched in total fascination while she carefully pulled long thin strips of bark off of a small willow tree. Gene was back at the car for his mid-afternoon bowl. He sure loved his weed. I never got into the stuff. Kali was now gathering her strips and carrying them to a corner of the hut. I wondered if it was some sort of nesting. I read another sign and learned that turkey vultures defecate on their legs to regulate their body temperature. I guess we all do what we gotta do to get by.

\*\*\*

The raucous girl gang texted me for karaoke that evening. I had a sitter anyway; I had a couple massages booked. I made the kids their favorite meal: roasted potatoes with sausage and peppers. I hugged them extra tight and read them an early story, since I would miss out on bedtime. The sitter was a life-saver, a retired school teacher who didn't mind late nights and lived a block away. She loved my children and they loved her. She'd quickly become almost like a grandma to them.

Client #1, I had seen before. He was the average middle-aged married guy. Gave me $120 every time and was super respectful. I enjoyed his conversation and easy nature.

Client #2 was new. I'd quoted him $150 when he initially inquired. I was experimenting with raising my prices. I was surprised when he agreed. When he arrived I had to wipe the shock off my face. He looked like Jon Cena. His face was handsome and friendly and his body was ridiculously ripped. I had never touched muscles like this before. Every part of his body was defined and hard to the touch. Why on earth would an Adonis like this need to pay for attention?

Jon Cena was also kind and flirty. He asked if I was

single. A lot of clients asked. I think most were just curious about how I lived my life. Jon Cena (yes, that is what I call him to this day) seemed interested in more than my story. I babbled about liking the single life and how my friends and I were going out when I finished with him. He grabbed my ass while I worked, pleasantly surprised by my habit of rarely if ever wearing panties. Usually I would gently remove the hand, and remind them of the 'no touching' rule. I let his be. He moaned sexily as I worked his muscles. I was exhausting all my strength to effectively get in there. It was a good workout. When I asked him to flip over, he turned, sat up, swept the hair from my neck, kissed it, and throatily whispered into my ear, "Please let me fuck you."

I shook my head and gently pushed him back down on the table. I worked his neck and massive shoulders and pecs letting my tits brush against his face. He playfully bit into one and I giggled. His erection proved his manhood was just as impressive as his physique. He groped my ass and chest the whole time I finished him off. It was tempting to jump up on the table and ride him, but that was a line I vowed to never cross.

After he'd recovered and dressed, he handed me a tiny baggie half full with white power. "A little tip for you." He said in his sexy, deep voice. I had, much wiser than when I started, collected payment before we got started. I gawked at the bag in disbelief.

"Is...is this coke?" I'd only seen it in movies. I don't even smoke pot and it's basically legal here! Despite my job, I was kind of a goodie-goodie. I'm the vice-president of the PTO! I haven't so much as received a parking ticket since I started driving! And now I was holding a bag of drugs.

"Sure," He smiled. "Have you ever tried it?"

"No. And I can't take it."

"Please do. It's all I have for a tip. Try it, you'll like it. That's enough to make sure you and your girlfriends have some fun tonight." He leaned forward and kissed my cheek. "I will be seeing you again. Soon."

Emboldened by that gorgeous man's interest, I gathered the girls into the bathroom when I arrived at the bar. I retrieved the baggie from my bra and waved it in the air. Almost as a war-cry I shouted: "Ladies, let's have some fun tonight."

## Chapter 7: If You Can't Say Anything Nice...

At the end of spring quarter, I was the happiest I'd been since my mom died. I had good friends and I was a good friend. I had made peace with Kennedy and trusted her with my secrets. K, as always, was supportive and loving. Although I felt like our family had changed greatly, the kids and I were excelling. My son was growing so fast, now 7 and remarkably smart. He'd been going by RJ lately, which I mostly hated but allowed. I'd named my children after my mother's parents Natalia and Rafeal Mercado. I'd never met them. They died before I was born. The names brought great pride to my mother.

Nat's punch-out had earned her a reputation of someone not to bother. Some older girls at the middle school took an interest in her. I'd met them; they were good kids - bookish and smart. Exactly the kind of people I wanted my daughter to befriend. She was always so shy. Until then, Nat only really hung out with one other kid, the neighbor girl she'd grown up with.

School was going well. I squeaked out a B+ in math and finally stood up to Professor HarasserDeWeirdo. I was also taking Spanish 202, but, uh, well, that was mostly for the easy A. ¡Claro hablo español, soy Latina!

Work was weird. The job didn't phase me at all anymore. I was almost clinical with my approach, but relaxed with clients. I started to see regulars in my home (there was space for the table in my bedroom with some rearranging) on my kidfree weekends. That saved me paying for hotels. I'd met them, repeatedly. Plus, there was the safety of good ol' MAD: Mutually Assured Destruction. I'd see Jon Cena client twice a month. It was almost impossible to resist his advances, but I managed. And masturbated furiously as soon as he left. I still could not fathom why he'd have to pay for release.

Especially from someone like me. I wasn't conventionally attractive. My hair was freaking awesome and I have good skin, but my eyebrows are unmanageable and I have thick thighs and hips. I have a little bit of belly I can't lose and nasty c-section scar. I have mom-arms that wiggle when I wave. My breasts were full but not huge and surprisingly pert for almost 32, but I had huge, dark pink nipples. Some men are attracted to my full lips and body. However, I would never be on a magazine cover.

Overall, we were happy and I was providing for us in a way that allowed me to be a full-time student, to volunteer at the elementary school, to take care of my pops, and to be there 100% for those who needed me. No other job would give me that level of flexibility and freedom.

I also had a new hobby. Or, more accurately, a new love for an old hobby. There was a cool, new brewery not far from my house. I am the worst Portlander - I think craft beer is gross and overpriced. On the rare occasion I want a cold beer, Dos Equis or PBR work just fine. That being said, a quality hard cider would always separate me from my money. Purists be damned; I always have it with a shot of Fireball. The brewery had 5-6 handles of its own brew and 30+ rotating from other local outfits. They used cute chalkboards they'd let customers decorate for signage of the different kinds. When I was free to spend the time, I would belly up to a delicious cider and carefully draw interesting signs. I was rusty on my lettering but I was still pretty good and it came back to me as I worked. Chalk's so easy to work with. I would include little illustrations with my special effect lettering. They were tiny masterpieces. After my second sign, I noticed I was no longer being charged for my ciders and they begged me to come in more often.

The loudest requests came from the cute hipster bartender, Marcus. He had a full, lush beard and a sleeve tattoo. He looked to be about 25. He smoothly asked for my number so he could text me when they needed a sign made. I told him to just light up the Bat-Signal.

He found me on facebook and started messaging me

often. He wasn't exactly thirsty, as the kids say. He was terribly flirty but not pushy. I kind of wanted him to ask me on a date but it never happened. Weeks of talking daily and seeing him at the pub but nothing more than flirting. I figured he had a girlfriend or something. Maybe I wasn't reading his signals correctly.

The last week of school, a week before my birthday, the ex-husband texted me to ask for a sit down talk. We had agreed during the divorce all serious conversations were to take place face-to-face. So much is lost in text. I had a great deal of anxiety when he arrived, these talks could go either way. We sat at the dining room table we'd purchased from a yard sale and test drove by possibly conceiving our son. We shot the shit for a few minutes and then he got serious and dropped the bomb.

"RJ wants to live with me."

Blood rushed to my ears and I could hear it swishing loudly. This could not be possible. Clearly, James had misunderstood the boy. I told James to hold on, to stop, but he kept talking. He insisted that Rafeal was afraid to tell me but had been asking for weeks. I could not believe what he was saying. Why would my son, my only son, the child I fed with my body, want to leave me? Obviously, James had talked him into this. I fought tears and excused myself to wash my face.

When I returned, his face was steeled in a stoic, blank expression, "Joe, I know this hard. But it's what the boy wants and it's what I want. I don't want to have to get lawyers involved, but I will."

My temper flared, "Then get one. You aren't taking my son. And get the fuck out of my house."

My courteous and respectful divorce was over. It was time for war.

***

I paced and practiced what I would say when Rafeal came home. He'd be late; he had Math is Cool practice today. I'd already arranged for his sister to hang out with the neighbor so he and I could talk in private. I needed to be cool and calm, an impossibility for me when I'm stressed. I already made a list of things I needed to do. I went nuclear on my laptop and deleted any and all evidence of my misdeeds. I hid my massage table under some old boxes in the shed. I went super private on my facebook and deleted all tagged pictures of me in bars or doing anything less than charity work.

I had a secret weapon. I knew a family lawyer. Intimately. And his wife certainly didn't know how well we knew each other. I scheduled an appointment with him the next day.

I scoured my house, top to bottom. It went from comfortably cluttered to magazine neat in 2 hours. Stress cleaning was my super-power.

When his adorable blond head came running in, I scooped him into a tight hug. He squealed and shouted that he had pee. I dropped him and allowed him to relieve himself. I had already put out a snack of milk and fresh cookies (from scratch - I stress bake too).

He came out and took his seat. He face was somber. "You talked to dad." Wow, he's getting so mature.

"Yes, mijo, I did." I was keeping it together. I reminded myself that it would be cruel for me ask this child to have responsibility of my emotions right now. I had to stay calm, for his sake as well as my own. "He told me that you want to live with him."

"Yeah." He offered quietly.

"Yeah, what? Is that true, Rafeal?"

"It's RJ! Please." His quiet was gone.

"I'm sorry, RJ. I don't understand why you don't like your name. It's a very popular name in-"

"In Puerto Rico." He interrupted with a sigh. "Yeah, I know. This ISN'T Puerto Rico, mom. This is America and HERE Rafeal is a Ninja Turtle and everyone makes fun of me. I hate it. And when I tell them it's Puerto Rican they call me the albino mexican. I'm sick of it. RJ is impossible to make fun of."

"I'm sorry," I said quietly, "I didn't know." I waited a few beats. "Is that why you want to move in with dad? Because of the teasing, you want to switch schools, maybe?" James now lived in a town 15 miles away with a different school district. He always wanted something more rural. I clung to my new theory. It wasn't me - it was the school.

"That's not it, mom." My hopeful heart broke again. What had I done?

"Can you tell me why?" I asked, trying to breathe.

"I just, I just want more time with dad." He took a big bite of his cookie. I waited.

"I want to spend a lot more time with dad." He continued after some milk. "I want to have a guy's house. Dad watches sport and listens to country music. He teaches me how to do guy stuff."

"Does it have to be living with him? What about just spending more time with him? Like maybe every weekend?" I guess I'd moved to bargaining.

"Dad doesn't want that. He wants me all the time." *UGH, I KNEW IT. James had put these ideas in his head! Of course a child would not choose to leave his mother all on his own. Calm it down, Joey.*

"Ok, sweets. I hear what you're saying. You'd like to watch sports over here? You'd like the house to be a little more guy-friendly?" At least my voice was sort of calm. I was desperate and trying my best.

"No, mom. That's not what I want. I want to LIVE with MY dad." He was solid, and again, so mature.

"Well, we can't decide this overnight. This will take time. And I am trying to listen and be respectful of what you want, but I'm not sure this is the right choice for you. ¿Comprende, mijo?"

He stood suddenly and reddened in the face, "This is America, mom. Speak English!" He ran to his room.

***

I hid in my room and fumed. My son's poor head was being filled with sexist, racist ideas from his stupid father! He wants a guy-house?! What in the actual fuck does that mean? Hating his name? Albino mexican? Was I suddenly in a Lynch film? Cause none of this garbage made a lick of sense.

My head spun from all the ideas going in a million directions. Where had I gone wrong? Was this karma? I had to get another job, something that will look good in court. I needed a conservative suit, no a sweater set. A motherly sweater set and pearls. My friend is a manager at Starbucks, I will apply first thing in the morning. I wished his Abuela was still alive. She'd beat some sense into him with her shoe. PUERTO RICO IS IN AMERICA! Kinda. I fell to my bed, my face in my hands, muttering, "What have I done? What will I do? Why? Why?"

***

A week later, James and I had another meeting. This time at our favorite diner. It was his weekend, and he would pick them up from my dad's house when he left. Peace had been made over phone calls and we both knew it was sensitive but urgent we talk it out. I knew what his lawyer had probably told him, the same thing mine had told me. "Work it out. You DO NOT want to go to court."

I went in with a low-ball offer in mind, and an acceptable middle I would agree to. I had talked to RJ a few more times and he was not budging. I wasn't going to force a kid to live somewhere he didn't want to be. There, at the diner where our family had countless pancakes, the day before my 32nd birthday, I gave away primary custody of my son.

***

I drove home and then walked to the pub. I would be having more than one cider.

Marcus stood at the bar, cleaning glasses when I walked in. He got the chalk out and grinned at me. I tried to smile back and asked for 3 shots with my cider. He raised his eyebrows but poured the drinks. I casually asked what signs needed making. He set down the drinks and excitedly handed me three chalkboards and a note from the manager specifying "Have Joelys draw signs for our new summer brews" and the details for each. It was flattering.

I drank and lettered and drank some more. I was on a mission to feel anything else. Marcus said something about how I was being so uncharacteristically quiet.

"Well, if you don't have anything nice to say…" I started. He didn't push.

The third sign wasn't quite up to my usual quality or originality, as I'd had more than a few by then. I warned Marcus that I may need a do-over.

"Any excuse to see me again, huh?" He said with a wink.

"Something like that." I shrugged. "Hey, Marcus?" I had a sudden rush of bravado. Or maybe just no longer gave any fucks.

"Hey, Joelys?" He leaned onto the bar.

"What time do you get off?"

## Chapter 8: Limon Pepino and Other Necessary Things

I woke with a hangover and a tattooed arm wrapped around me. The drinking and the sex helped me forget how much I hurt, but all that energy rushed back to me as my eyes adjusted to the light. I leapt out of my bed and ran into my bathroom, purging what I could.

I usually don't drink much and rarely to get drunk. Well, that was most of my adult life. The last year had certainly been different. My mama was a drunk and the possibility of history repeating was terrifying. I splashed water on my face and mentally started to a to-do list. Drink water, kick the hipster out, tidy room, massage at...damn, what time? I needed my phone. I had a really busy day planned. I chugged two glasses of water, brushed my teeth, and tidied my hair.

Returning to my room, I searched for clothes. Marcus shifted in my bed and moaned slightly. He had the 'dad bod': thick thighs and a belly but solid arms. I remembered the sex to be alright. Not great. I threw on last night's dress when I found it on the floor and made some coffee. I fed the asshole cat while I waited for it to brew. The window showed a perfect June morning, clear skies and lush green leaves. Portland is weird in good weather. Well, Portland is always weird, it's part of our pathos. But sunshine really brings out the freaks. I pour entirely too much white mocha raspberry creamer into a mug and topped it some coffee. I poured another with a reasonable amount of creamer and carried them into my bedroom.

Sitting quietly on my bed, I checked my phone. It was 9:10 and I had massages booked for 10am, noon, and 3:30pm. The last one wouldn't be a massage. It was the gym-going guy from my very first weekend. He'd been grandfathered in, against my normal rules, and met with me for $200 blow jobs once or twice a month. I had pedicures with girls at 5pm and then everyone was coming back here for my party. Having solidified my schedule and needing to get started, I roused the beardo snoring lightly in my bed.

Marcus did not slink away as I'd hoped. When I gently shook him, he reached up and bear hugged me back to a snuggle position. I shifted and he gripped harder. His eyes never opened. I pushed with more force and said, "Really, dude, you need to get up." Groaning in protest, he sat up a little. I asked if he'd like some coffee and he grunted a yes. I told him I hated to be rude, but I had a very busy day that needed to start now.

"Sure," He said sarcastically. "You're just trying to get me outta here."

"Yes, I am. Because I have a busy day and I need to get going."

He didn't budge. "Whatcha got goin' on?" He sipped the coffee and complimented the yummy creamer.

"Thanks, it's my favorite." I paused, unsure of what

and how much to tell him. I went for it. "I have a massage client coming in less than an hour. I have to shower and tidy before he gets here. I have two other clients and I have to get the house ready for a party."

"A party? What for?"

I gazed blankly at the wall behind him and softly offered, "My birthday. Today's my birthday."

***

The day was, thankfully, a blur of activity. Between my clients, cleaning, and preparing food and a drink station for the party, I hardly had time to think. I went all out and strung all the Christmas lights haphazardly across the ceiling and hung a disco ball I had purchased ages ago for Nat's 5th birthday (her weird disco phase). I made two playlists, one for mellow conversation and one for a rumpus. At our age, it could still go either way. I picked the perfect dress: a short, bright red number that looked amazing against my newly blue hair. The facebook event claimed over 30 people people were coming. The girls were clamoring through my door as just finished stocking the bathroom.

These women were loud and fun and I was so lucky to have found them. They all started talking at once and it was chaos. Oakley took charge, as usual.

Oakley was not her birth name. At seven-years-old, she was such a crack shot her family dubbed her 'Annie Oakley' and the latter part stuck. She still shoots competitively. She was the perfect mix of feminine and masculine in a sexy way: with a generous hour-glass figure and long, dark hair but also never shy or timid, she was quick to remind people that she was in-charge. She chewed tobacco (YUCK!) and bow-hunted, but also could apply perfect eye-liner and always wore a gorgeous shade of red lipstick. We'd grown close lately and I'd learned she was also incredibly bright and thoughtful. She was constantly surprising me with articulate, well-thought ideas about world events. Having been acquaintances for five years, I had regretfully dismissed her a yet another lame redneck chick before I got to know her.

Next to Oakley was a another girl I'd known for years but only grew close to recently, Courtney Heller. I would never tell Courtney this, but I was insanely jealous of her and wrongly assumed she would be a stuck-up bitch. She was unbelievably gorgeous. Huge, sapphire eyes framed by dark, thick lashes and full, perfect lips. Shiny, curly hair that always looked amazing. She was a curvy, thick girl, but rocked it in a way that turned heads. If that wasn't enough, she was literally the most talented singer I'd ever heard. Her version of Cohen's Hallelujah would make a karaoke bar lose its mind. It turns out, on top of being super talented and beautiful, Court was generous and sweet.

Attached at Courtney's hip was alway Cat Holding. Also sweet and generous, Cat is the stereotypical ditzy blonde. She's a total sweetheart, always happy. However, well, sometimes she doesn't have the best memory. Or logic. And she was super flakey. Her sweetness made any fault completely forgivable. Cat's the friend that can sense when you're having a bad day and magically show up with your favorite coffee. She's the only one of our group that isn't single, however, that was debatable to me. Cat's been engaged for a few years, but I've never so much as seen a picture of her fiance. Courtney and Cat had been best friends since elementary school and it was beyond adorable.

The girls had brought champagne and orange juice for celebratory mimosas before we went for our planned pedicures. We giggled through the bottle while I regaled them with my adventures with bartender from the night before (an exaggeration, it was pretty lame sex). They gave me the perfect distraction from my grief.

\*\*\*

I woke with a hangover and a tattooed arm wrapped around me.

Wait, was it yesterday? My pounding head struggled to make sense of the surroundings. Had I invited Marcus to the party? I vaguely remembered texting him after I had several shots. My whole body hurt. I groaned.

Marcus pulled me closer and kissed the back of my neck. He whispered roughly that he knew what I needed. I felt his erection against my ass and I started to protest but then didn't care. He angled my body awkwardly on my side and roughly jammed his cock all the way in. I wasn't ready, dehydrated, and it hurt. I still didn't care. He jackrabbit-fucked me for two solid minutes and came, collapsing his heavy body over mine. Panting, he barked, "You have the tightest pussy babe. Damn."

I excused myself to bathroom. I needed to puke and shower. I heard him making some noise, moving around. I hoped he was leaving. The door opened and I heard the toilet seat hit the back of the tank. I yelled over the curtain, "There's another bathroom in the hall!"

"Some hipster dude is in there." It wasn't Marcus. I peeked, and saw Gene taking a leak. I had never seen him without pants. Not bad. I pulled the curtain back quickly and apologized. He laughed.

"I crashed on Raf's bed. There's some of your girl gang here too." He was being vague because he had a huge crush on Courtney but it wasn't happening. I made a note to inform her of my new insider information. He continues, "You feel as shitty as me?"

"Ohhh, dude. I will NEVER drink like that again." I was now sitting in the tub, standing proved too hard. "Do you think you could see if I have any Gatorade?"

"Ten steps ahead, birthday girl. An Uber will be delivering some in about 10 minutes." Damn, Gene was cool.

"Did you get-" I started

"Limon Pepino, your weird favorite. And a variety of others. I didn't know what the Lady Mafia prefered. Or your lumberjack."

"He's not my anything." I protested but Gene was already gone.

An hour or so later it was just Oakley, Gene, and me. Courtney and Cat had helped to cleaned up a bit, but bailed to get some more sleep in their own beds. Marcus slipped out while I was in the shower. I sipped my coffee infused creamer and picked at the breakfast burrito I made. It was cold and I wasn't hungry. The others had inhaled them, exclaiming them to be the best tasting food they'd ever had. I knew that was hyperbole, but I also do a tasty secret step. I saute the onions and peppers in the bacon grease.

I was grateful they stayed. It was time to share the news of my family's upheaval. They listened patiently and held me while I sobbed. Gene had some insights, being a son whose parents had divorced. I felt a little better, having people in my corner to help me carry it all.

I could not face the kid pick-up that day. I could not, under any circumstance, go pick up my daughter and leave my son. Gene volunteered to do it and I started crying again, but this time with gratitude. I had no idea what I would do without him. Oakley said we still had a couple hours and if I wasn't driving, I should have some hair of the dog. I knew that was a terrible choice but I didn't care. I needed to feel something other than the emptiness of loss.

**Chapter 9: Kindly Fuck Off**

I attacked life with every bit of energy I could muster in my 32nd year. At first, I was determined to fix whatever I had done to break my relationship with my son. To be a person he could be proud of and want to live with. I spent endless hours cleaning and organizing my house. I tried not to push or make a big deal around RJ. I also realized I was showering him with presents and giving into his every whim. I can't buy him. That's not healthy. I curbed the behavior quickly. Nat benefited from my guilt as well so I hoped there wasn't too much damage.

I scored a barista position at a coffee kiosk in a large box store. I still worked my other gig. More than ever - I needed money. My child support had been cut by half and now I owed child support to James for RJ. Because of the income difference, he still owed a bit more than me so I now received $205/month, less than a 1/4th of what I used to get. I'm not complaining, fair is fair, but it was a huge and sudden loss of income. Especially during summer break, when I had no financial aid.

We were on the summer modified parenting plan, which meant the kids hung out with me during the day and their dad picked him them up after work. We'd still alternate weekends. It was a good plan, rather than either of us paying for childcare. It meant I got to see RJ almost every day and that felt awesome. I held hope that if I tried hard enough, when fall came he'd change his mind about the move. My nights free to work either job, I was keeping up financially too.

Dating sites like plentyoffish and OkCupid were helping to occupy my free time and my bed. Let's just say I wasn't lonely much.

I low-key hated the barista job. My friend had helped me get it, but unfortunately not at her location. Instead my boss was 22-years-old and a micro-managing megalomaniac. I fumed internally when she spent 5 minutes showing me how to open a box. I even kept it together when she called that a 'teachable moment'. I was only hired for 12 hours a week, three shifts of four hours. The paychecks hardly felt worth it, but I needed the documented income, in case things got legal with the ex. I hated working the bar, the steam made it hot and uncomfortable, especially with the aprons and dumb visors we were forced to wear. Oh, and pants. The uniform required black pants. My ass and thighs were not made for pants. Even forgiving yoga pants involved near constant tugging in the back to keep from exposing my crack. Working at a location in a grocery store, I had to join a union and wear these super expensive, ugly-as-fuck, non-slip shoes (which the union graciously sold to me for $55).

There were good parts too. I liked working the register and talking to the customers. My coffee game had improved at home (still drowned in creamers, though). But the best part was the signage. I got to design and write out the daily specials and offers on four signs in and outside the store. I was given a drawer of chalk markers and free reign once the manager saw my talent. Customers started taking pictures of my work and I would see them tagged on social media.

My other job was busier than ever, despite raising my prices. I'd also worked out a deal with a front desk employee at the area's nicest hotel. He passed my number on to inquiring potential clients and I gave him a free massage every month - just a massage, he was super gay and had sciatica. My massages were excellent, my arms now Herculean strong. I took that part seriously, often watching tutorials and educational videos on techniques I hadn't learned or forgotten. I purchased hot stones and towel warmer to give it a more spa like experience. Months before, I'd looked into getting my license to maybe go legit. None of the education I had prior would count and I'd have to start over. A year's time and 5 grand to get paid less for what I was already doing. No thanks.

I was also fighting immense anger. I had, on some levels, been angry since the day James walked out, but it was quicker to surface now. He promised, in front of his whole family and the God in which he believes, to love, honor, and cherish me until one of us died. I ain't dead motherfucker. The cherish was the first to go, the love was hanging in there for 8 years or so, but the honor left the night he packed that bag. The only reason he agreed to the thoughtful and kind divorce was the fact that he couldn't afford the alternative.

It wasn't just James. I wasn't just my pushy boss, Vonda DeControlFreak. It wasn't the situation with RJ. It wasn't my clients, not even the pushy ones. I hated the douches on the dating sites, but it wasn't even their fault. I woke angry, I fought it every moment of the day. The anger was deep inside me. I tried not to explore the causation too much, but I was growing suspicious that the anger was toward my mother. Or maybe I was born angry and it was just now manifesting.

I wasn't sleeping much. James would drop the monkeys off at 5:50AM and they'd always be starving. Rather than listen to them bitch while I cooked, I started waking at 5:30 to have it ready by the time they got there. Some mornings I would just buy donuts and sleep in, but I loved the luxury of a nice sit-down morning meal with my favorite people more than I loved sleep. We'd spend the day doing our favorite stuff: playing games, watching movies, hitting the public pool, or sometimes the zoo. Their dad would pick them up around 5 and I would head to one job or the other. The coffee stand closed at 10 but I'd book massages as late as 2 or 3 in the morning. My clients appreciated my flexibility. Even when I got to bed at a reasonable time, sleep eluded me. The anger welled up, and I couldn't find peace.

\*\*\*

Dad's health still precarious, I was now checking on him daily. His spirits were high but a simple task like checking the mailbox across the street would wear him out for the whole day. It didn't stop him from trying of course, the old mule. He was still smoking a pack a day and drinking a half a handle a night. He was still playing cards with the boys on Friday nights. He was still my pops, just a much slower version.

The kids and I were doing our daily check-in when I noticed the yellow in his eyes. I told the kids to go set the sprinklers in the backyard and sat down next to him. I asked if he'd noticed his jaundice and he shrugged and suggested it was the poor lighting in the house. I said we needed to go to the doctor and he told me to kindly fuck off. After all the stress, after the countless nights of watching my mother writhe in pain, after endless days of wiping her ass and shrugging off her emotional abuse: it looked likely that I would be doing the same with dad. The pit of anger in my stomach grew.

\*\*\*

That Friday, after the kids were picked up for their weekend with James and after I had serviced a couple clients, the girls came over for pre-gaming and hair and make-up. It had become a fun tradition on nights out: getting pretty together and having a few drinks to cut down on a the bar bill. Our social life mostly centered around karaoke. I was no Courtney, but I'd always loved singing. My alto voice was best for Amy Winehouse songs and classic rock covers. I envied how Courtney and Oakley could rock pretty much any song they tried. Cat didn't sing, she just liked the show. And the booze.

I confided in them the anger I'd been feeling. They all reacted with different advice. Oakley is a fixer, and her analytical brain listed ways I could reduce my stress. Courtney is empathetic and spiritual and suggested meditation. Cat said we needed shots.

\*\*\*

I woke with a hangover and a tattooed arm wrapped around me.

Jesus, I needed to block Marcus. Alcohol gave me some sort of bad sex amnesia.

\*\*\*

I was still feeling rough when I got to the coffee stand that evening. I was extra grumpy because if I hadn't had to work that shift, I could have booked two clients at $150 a piece. I was able to rebook one, but was missing out on the cash from the other to make $8.35/hr, shared tips. Vonda VonBossyPants was instantly on my ass when I walked in. Evidently, I was marking boxes on the drink cups with check marks instead of an 'X'. An unforgivable offense.

An hour into my shift, HR came by with our paychecks. We were in a lull with no customers, so I peeked to see how much I'd earned. Vonda La'NeedsALaxative appeared from nowhere and had a 'teachable moment' with me about how we needed to clean when there were no customers (I was literally on my way to grab the broom when HR stopped me). Hearing her drone on while I saw the total of $87.20, wages minus taxes, social security, and my union fees, I lost control. Eighty-seven bucks was not worth my time or this bitch's attitude. I removed my apron and told Vonda to kindly fuck off.

I was home in time to contact and rebook the client I would have missed. I made a mental note to donate half of the proceeds from this massage to the Women's Resource Center or the YWCA. I could not imagine my life if I had to support my kids on minimum wage.

\*\*\*

After the client - a respectful older man who tipped me too much - left I logged on to plentyoffish. I'd been corresponding with a sandy-haired, rugged man named Danny. He seemed smart and interesting. A divorcee and year older than me, we seemed pretty evenly matched. He mentioned that he was in town for the evening (his circumstances were unique to say the least). I asked him if he wanted to bring a bottle over and get weird. He was knocking on my door 20 minutes later.

Some people were put on this earth to heal or perform amazing surgeries. Some people are here with the gift of humor and bring us endless joy and laughter. Musicians born to move and inspire others. Teachers, dancers, mathematicians, gardeners: every single person was put on this planet with a gift to share. Danny McCrea was born to fuck women.

I'd had great lovers before. I'd never met a man as talented and insatiable as Danny. His tall body was toned but soft and his, ahem, biology was gifted. Though it was more than that, his huge hands somehow were always hot to the touch and exactly where I wanted them. He played my body like a master pianist can attack and execute Beethoven. I was overwhelmed with the passion and intensity of the sex I shared with this man.

Completely satisfied, I feel asleep peacefully in his arms. I felt safe and calm: emotions almost foreign to me at that point.

**Chapter 10: Someone to Watch Over Me**

By mid-summer, Danny and I were an official couple. It was not our intention; it had happened almost by accident. I was completely comfortable with us hooking up a few times and parting ways. In fact, we'd happily agreed to super casual as neither of us were in a good place for a relationship. They say life is what happens when you're busy making plans.

Danny lived in the middle of the woods, helping with his family's lumber business. His cabin was an hour's drive away from my house. Now here's a little fun fact about Joelys Jeffries: I do not do nature. I'm indoorsy.

I like air conditioning and high speed internet. The most miserable moments of my life have been spent hiking and camping. The great outdoors is just not for this girl. I've always felt a bit guilty about that. I live in a nature-lover's paradise and it's completely wasted on me. Ideally, I would have sexy times at my place, in my comfortable bed, where there are absolutely no bears. However, Danny needed to stay close to his home.

His father was dying.

His mother was caring for the man, but needed Danny near for heavy lifting and emotional support. The whole family lived on the property, his brother's family and his sister. So, if I wanted to have Danny, which I desperately needed to do as often as possible, I had to drive to his place and deal with the woods. And the bears.

I am not being hyperbolic. The first time I traversed his insanely long, bumpy driveway, there was a cinnamon bear just chillin' out. I called Danny, panicked. He walked over and chased it away with a broom. It was the dumbest, scariest, hottest thing I'd ever seen in real life. After a few weeks of regular meet-ups, again no feelings or strings, his father passed away.

The death forever bound me to Danny. His father died the same way I lost my mother. The two had drank themselves to the grave before 60-years-old. I was uniquely qualified to help him cope. The night they had to call the coroner, I made the trek to his property. I wasn't sure what was appropriate to bring, so I brought everything. An orchid for his mother, a casserole, a cheesecake, and couple bottles of Jameson - the family patriarch's prefered brand. The family appreciated the food and drinks and thoughtful gestures. Danny was only interested in an almost destructive ownership of my body.

After three or maybe four rounds of relentless, exhausting sex, his dick finally stopped cooperating. I spread out on his bed, assessing the damage. He laid his head on my chest and the stillness and the quiet of the moment caught up to him and he began to gently sob. I gently rubbed and patted his back and gave him a safe place to let go.

In the morning I made breakfast for the whole compound and tried to help his mother with whatever she could ask of me. I'd let Danny sleep in. I didn't sleep at all, pine cones and squirrels kept bombarding the metal roof and I felt like I was in a war zone. I wanted to help this family, their grief so similar to my own. When they started to plan the wake, Danny's sister, Irene, half-jokingly suggest I cater. She had devoured most of my cheesecake and declared it the best she'd ever had. I'd catered some events in the past: a friend's wedding, a few showers, my mother's wake, I wasn't phased by the idea of cooking for a big crowd. I offered my services and the family readily accepted.

At the wake, held at this gorgeous resort cabin by Mt. Hood, Danny's mom and Irene kept grabbing me out of the kitchen and introducing me to extended family and friends as, "Danny's girlfriend, Joelys." They sang my praises, "This is Joelys, Danny's girlfriend. She made all the food! Did you try her cheesecakes?" It was overwhelming but flattering. Later, I found Danny sitting alone in the cabin's loft. The place was enormous, the loft area had 10 or so twin beds in a row. He was sitting on the one closest to the window, staring out into the blue sky. I quietly let him know I was there and asked if he needed anything.

"No, I'm good." he said, emotionlessly. "Come sit, if you'd like."

The food was all prepared. People downstairs had been fed and were now hitting the drinks. I sat.

"I made sure your mom ate something." I reassured him. "She really likes the meatballs." I didn't know what to say.

"I heard you're my girlfriend." He said with a chuckle.

"Yeaaaaaaahhh," I drew out, making a pensive face, "I didn't want to correct them, it was super awkward."

"Then don't." He was pulling my uncharacteristically demure black dress up my thighs and knelt between my legs. "Joe!" He started sternly, "Did you forget to wear panties to my father's wake?"

"Oops!" I giggled and his mouth pressed against the outer lips of my soft labia. His tongue entered them purposefully and I gasped.

Moments later I was suppressing my climax into a pillow. I couldn't believe what we had just done. Before I could say anything his pants were off and his cock was in my mouth, growing harder. Once he was rock hard, he masterfully pulled me up and bent my body over in one smooth motion. He slowly slid his whole length in me and held it there for while. He bent over and whispered in my ear, "This is my pussy now." He started rocking his hips forcibly and pumping in and out, accentuating each thrust with another claim of me and my womanhood. "My pussy" Thrust, push. "My woman." Slamming harder. "You belong to me, now Joe." Faster. "You're mine." Some mix of the weird possessive talk, the inappropriate location, and his animalist want for me made me come harder than I ever thought possible.

\*\*\*

That night in one of the cabin rooms, we laid tangled together after somehow finding the energy to have sex again. He kissed my cheek and asked if I was happy.

"I feel like there's no good answer," I said. "Yeah, that was some fine fucking, but we're at your father's wake." He laughed.

"I think we could be happy. I've never met a woman who could keep up with me before. And," He laughed again, "my family loves you." He waited a beat. "You wanna do this thing?"

"Do this thing?!" I teased. "So romantic."

"I'll show you romantic." He declared as he parted my thighs with his shoulders and started kissing down my tummy. It occurred to me, much later, I never really said yes.

\*\*\*

The rest of the summer and the fall were a manic blur of fucking and living life to the fullest. I never slept. I didn't care. I was addicted to Danny.

We went hard at everything, not just each other's genitals. We partied hard, countless nights of shots and lines of coke and dancing and singing. He introduced the kids and me to rafting and kayaking. On my weekends the kids would camp out on his property and ride his 4-wheelers. We took a trip to the beach and he built us a giant bonfire. The anger inside me was fading or at least hiding. Every moment with him was something new for me, something completely out of my comfort-zone.

Having learned my lesson, painfully, I was completely honest with him about my job. He didn't care. He thought it was hot. He'd have me tell him details of the men and their dicks during our foreplay. We'd agreed to be open. I was hesitant but game to try something new. Also, with my occupation, it was a little bit of a requirement. We were laying in my bed, a rare night at my place. His mom was still in a great deal of pain and he didn't like to leave her alone often. He asked about the clients I would be seeing later. I grinned and told him it was Jon Cena Client day.

I explained my attraction to the bulky man, which was weirdly freeing and sexy to share with this other man I cared for. Danny excitedly said, "Oh, you've got to fuck this guy."

"I wish." I smiled. "But, I have to have these boundaries. For my sanity."

"No, not for money. Just finish the massage and the

sex is separate." He gave me a pleading look, his soulful eyes intent. "I think it would be the hottest thing I could ever listen to. I'll hang out in your bathroom, he'll never know." For extra measure he added, "Please?"

"I thought this was *your* pussy." I raised my eyebrow at him.

"Damn right." He asserted, grabbing it roughly. "And I can share it if I want."

I acquiesced. Four hours later I was massaging Jon Cena Client. I flirted and teased and drove the man wild. At one point, I saw my bathroom door crack open and Danny sneak a quick peek. I was a little reluctant to go through with our plan. It really did violate my rules. And it didn't seem fair to Jon (I honestly don't know his real name). He didn't consent to this. The hesitation did not stop me, when I had Jon flip over and he flirtingly asked me when I was going let him have my pussy - I said, "Now." And I kissed him, slipping out of my skimpy dress and leading him to the bed where Danny would have a better view.

It was over as quickly as it started. Twenty, maybe thirty, seconds of jack-rabbit pounding and he pulled out and came all over my stomach and tits. He collapsed beside me, panting at how great it was. I smiled, not sure what to say. Poor guy, he never had to try at this, did he? He asked me why I had changed my mind. I wasn't sure. I finally said, "I couldn't handle not knowing how it felt to fuck you." He seemed pleased with my answer and got dressed. I stayed on the bed, watching his jizz drizzle down my side. He threw another couple bills on the massage table and leaned down to kiss my cheek before he let himself out.

The front door hadn't even fully closed when Danny rushed out the of the bathroom, already naked and so erect his dick was reddish purple. He was all over me, on me, in me, kissing me everywhere. He scooped up a fingerful of the other's man's load and told me to lick it off. I was trying to be present, this was all very sexy, but my mind kept wandering to the bills on the table. Jon had already paid me, $150 on my desk. That cash on the table means I was just paid for sex. I was officially a prostitute.

\*\*\*

Knowing I was a rather upset over my newest job title (yes, I stuck on the semantics. Clearly, it wasn't a big leap for me, but it was the one line I thought I would never cross), Danny asked me to take a night off from my responsibilities for a special date. The only instruction he gave me was to wear something pretty and drive out to his property at 6pm.

I purchased a new dress, a twirly, full-skirted, retro, black one with white polka dots and a sweetheart neckline. I felt pretty and oh-so feminine. I paired it with my favorite cashmere cardigan, kitten heels, a matte red lip and headed his way. I parked in my normal spot, curious as to what he had planned. I knew he was pretty broke, most of his family's timber money going toward new equipment to keep up with the bigger outfits. He walked out of his cabin, his tall frame looking extraordinarily handsome in a suit. Hair slicked back, he gave me his best, sexy smirk. I melted a little.

He escorted me to his 4-wheeler, freshly washed. I joked about being a bit overdressed and he told me not to worry. We rode for about 15 minutes, my arms wrapped around his waist, to a gorgeous meadow I'd not seen before. He pulled up to the scene he'd set up for us: a little table and two chairs and a full bed. The bed had a platform and what looked to be 10 thick blankets. The table was set with candles and a white, lace tablecloth. He helped me off my seat and led me to the table. I noticed there was a little smoldering fire on the other side of the table and an ice chest. He took my hand, "Drink, my dear?"

"Oh, twist my arm." I laughed into the beauty of the scene. I couldn't believe all the effort this must have taken. He reached into the cooler and pulled out two champagne flutes and bottle of Andre. I giggled. I can honestly say I would never know the difference between it and Dom. He expertly navigated the foil and the cork and poured us two generous servings.

"A toast:" He started, "To love and and to the ridiculous things it makes us do." I cheers'd with a grin.

"Oh, music!" He suddenly remembered, turning toward an older 90s boombox set on a tree stump. Ella Fitzgerald's 'Someone to Watch Over Me' appeared in the void of the meadow as his long, strong arm wrapped around my waist. "Dance?" I downed my drink and set the glass gently on the table. How on earth could I resist?

After a lovely dinner of salmon and vegetables, brilliantly cooked in foil packets, we danced and drank some more. The sky turned dark while we celebrated the beauty and each other. He stoked to the fire to keep us warm. It was September, the nights get pretty cold. The music of Ella and Duke and Louis and Frank eventually gave way to the crickets and owls and frogs from a small pond nearby. We took to the bed.

I had never seen a sky like that before. Away from light pollution, the night seemed endless and the countless stars created angelic, surreal light all around us. He was kissing my neck while I saw a shooting star and I wished to always remember the events and emotions of this night. And then I saw two more. I pointed up, speechless. "Aww," Danny whispered, "It's later than I thought." The next 30 minutes we laid naked in each other's arms, wrapped in the coziest nest of blankets, watching the most incredible meteor shower I have ever or will ever see. When it was almost over, and the sheer quantity of bright beams slowed, we exchanged 'I love you's for the first time.

Our cries of passion soon joined the crickets and night birds as we made love in the magic of that meadow.

***

Danny wanted a threeway. I'd never been with a woman before, but it seemed pretty hot. I was looking into booking us professional when he told me he found Courtney to be very sexy and asked if it could be with her. I was dumbfounded. And a little jealous.

He talked me into it in that way he could talk me into anything. I hinted at it with her and she seemed as reluctant as I was. He worked his mojo on her a few nights later, all of us drinking at my place. He gave her a neck rub and I tried to calm my heart. I'm not sure what he whispered in her ear, but she got up from her chair and kissed me. It was bizarre to feel feminine lips on mine. And then Danny was pulling us up and toward my bedroom.

Quelling the jealousy, I watched his huge, hot hands undress my friend. I wasn't sure what to do. I started kissing his neck and they both took my dress off. As usual, I wasn't wearing anything under it. Court was a little more work, leggings and boots and a vest. I steadied myself. I knew Danny really wanted to see me go down on my friend. I worried I would be bad at it. I have a rough I idea of the general anatomy, but I worried my tongue would be too short or not strong enough. I reminded myself that even bad oral sex still felt pretty good. My fears were interrupted by Courtney, one of my closest friends, softly pushing me down and crawling between my thighs.

**Chapter 11: The Fish and the Bird**

The rest of September was weird and super fast. Danny and I survived the threesome, but I worried my friendship with Court had not. She acted like everything was fine, but I was seeing much less of her. I'm sure she told Cat, who was also hardly talking to me. I had little time to worry about it, between Fall quarter at school and my father's declining health.

Having learned my lesson caring for my mother, I found him the perfect home health aide, Jason.

Basically homeless (couch surfing), Jason was grateful to be paid in room, board, weed, and smokes. He had experience with care-giving, his little brother had tragically died of ALS two years prior. Dad was resistant to the change until Jason picked up Leeroy Jeffries' signature 12-string and played it like it had been his birthright. I checked on them daily and would usually find them jamming on various instruments, getting high, and having a grand ol' time. Jason also managed to get dad to doctor's appointments with minimal fuss. I couldn't find the right amount of gratitude for this saint of a man.

We'd survived Nat's 13th birthday. She had no demands or giant aspirations, just not too many people and a pinata. Using Oakley's connections, we got a pretty badass karaoke system set up and I asked Kennedy's cute 17-year-old cousin, Jess, to 'bartend' the ice cream float bar. It was a smash hit with Nat and her friends. My dad constructed her an elaborate dragon pinata. It was almost painful to watch it get smashed, but Nat saved the beast's head.

A week later, at the start of my kid-free weekend, I canceled plans with Danny because a lingering head cold had me feeling like absolute garbage. I just needed sleep which was impossible with him around. He surprised me with a knock on the door, in his hands: flowers, whiskey, honey, and tea. I was beyond touched. A couple of hot toddies later, I was sleeping deeply in his arms.

My clogged sinuses woke me early, 5AM. I tried a shower and a decongestant but I was miserable. The coughing and clamour woke Danny too. He made me another sweet, strong toddy and some coffee for himself. We sat in my bed and talked. My asshole cat jumped up to yell at us for a couple minutes. I don't know if it was the hour or the fact that we rarely just sat and talked but for the first time in our short, intense relationship things got serious and heavy. He asked if I would be willing to have more children.

"This might be my least favorite subject." I told him. "I can't have more. Medically can't."

"Would you have more kids, though?" He pressed. "If you could, or maybe adopt or through surrogacy?" I had remembered once when he was playing with RJ he told me he couldn't wait for a son of his own.

"Honestly, I would be really hesitant. I've repopulated the planet enough. Plus, that baby phase is awful, I'm finally in that place where my kids are awesome and can have real conversations." I knew I wasn't telling him what he wanted to hear, but I had to be clear where I stood.

After some shared silence and sipping, he asked, "Where do you see us in a few years?"

I couldn't say I hadn't thought about it. But, I also knew he wouldn't like my answer.

We talked some more, both of us realizing the futility of our love. I liked the vacation from reality found in visits to his wooded home, but I would hate to live there. He loved it. He wouldn't want to live anywhere else. I actually wanted, eventually, to live somewhere more urban. He wanted more children. I, clearly, did not. We paused the serious talk to make love one last time, a farewell fuck. Both of us realized that early morning - a fish and a bird can fall in love, but where would they live?

\*\*\*

He left around 7AM. I grabbed the bottle of whiskey, took a big swig, while snapping a selfie. My hair was frightful, my skin a trainwreck from being sick and crying. I sent the pic to Oakley with the caption: Guess who's single again?

She was up, texting me back right away. "OMG! You ok?"

"Yeah, I'll live." I tapped back.

"Are you still coming today? Want me to pick you up?"

Shiiiiiit. I had forgotten about Redneck Days. Oakley was going to be singing with this country band at this awful/awesome bar out in Beaverton. She said it was going to be super fun. I asked her what time I should be ready.

The locals took Redneck Days seriously. There was Chicken Shit Bingo (yes, with real chickens) and a lawnmower race. I mostly sat on a hay-bale, taking it all in. People had blacked out teeth and there were so very many sets of overalls. I wasn't sure what to wear, but as I told Oakley, I started drinking Jack Daniels at 7AM - I was a true redneck today.

\*\*\*

I woke with a hangover and a tattooed arm wrapped

around me.

Marcus?! What in the actual fuck? I hadn't talked to him in months. I think I misjudged the safety of decongestants and drinking; I don't even remember Oakley's performance with the band. I had no idea how I got home or how he...damn. I stumbled to the bathroom.

\*\*\*

Gene was my only friend still talking to me in October. I'd really goofed things up Oakley, making a scene at Redneck Days. I blacked out most of it, but heard rumors that I had liberated the chickens and caused chaos. Marcus told me when he got there (I had, evidently, insisted he come join us), I was being pulled out of the bar and calling them all racist. And then I raised my dress and mooned the whole crowd, telling them to kiss my big, Puerto Rican ass.

I wanted to reach out to Kennedy, but so much had happened and she'd missed out on so much. She only made a brief appearance at Nat's birthday and it was super awkward. I knew I had been hanging out with my new friends way more than her, but she didn't seem to like going out anymore. Plus, she was trying to get pregnant and it was literally all she talked about. I dropped off a card and her favorite chocolate in her mailbox, telling her I loved and missed her. She texted me to thanks but didn't invite me over or ask to see me.

I had reached out to Oakley, Courtney, and Cat as well. They promised me we were cool, but it didn't seem like it.

Gene had big news one morning. He'd gotten an incredible job with a tech company in IT support. The pay was a great deal more than cooking and it being a 'real' job there were benefits and vacation time. The only bummer was that he'd no longer be able to drive me to school. I totally understood; I was super proud of him. We celebrated his last day of 'freedom' with one of our fun adventures. We went to The Dalles and found a couple decent thrift shops and a damn good tavern burger.

***

I woke with a hangover and a tattooed arm wrapped around me.

What was this, fucking Groundhog's Day? I pieced together the events from the night prior. My phone was ringing. It was Nat; I was late to pick her up from her dad's.

***

I was having already having the shittiest morning when Jason called. There was no on-campus parking and I had to walk over mile in the freezing November fog. I'd done poorly on my chem exam. James had been nasty with me via text because I asked if I could have RJ an extra night. Jason was in tears and I knew what he was going to say.

My father had died that morning, peacefully in his chair with an Irish coffee in his hand.

\*\*\*

When I was six, I asked my dad how a light bulb worked. Hours later, we were surrounded in papers on living room floor. He'd mapped out the whole cycle of electricity for me, from the coal plant to the light bulb's filament, in intricate drawings and diagrams.

When I was 12, I really wanted to go to the school's sock hop, but the costume store was out of poodle skirts. He took me to the craft store and we sewed one by hand. He taught me how to embroider and my skirt was 10 times nicer than the other girls'.

When I was 18, sharing my first whiskey with my father, Fourth of July, sitting on our lawn watching the fireworks: he told me that I was the best thing he'd ever done with his life.

As much as I tried to prepare for this moment, I was not ready to lose him. I was completely and irrevocably devastated.

**Chapter 12: Loss**

I now had two urns and no parents. Mom left very specific instructions for her remains, but I had yet to carry out her wishes. I asked my father once and he said, "Fuck it. Flush me; I'll end up at the ocean eventually." I had no intention of following those commands.

Mom wanted her ashes taken to Puerto Rico and spread over the graves of her mother, father, and brother. I had a million excuses as to why I hadn't completed the task yet, but bottom line, I simply wasn't ready. I suppose it would be fitting to spread dad's with mom's, keeping them together. I would have to back burner this again; there's no way I could afford that trip. I sighed, I had to ready for my father's wake.

Hosting at my home was stressful, but the cooking, cleaning, and busy work kept me sane. I wore a replica of the poodle skirt he'd made me so many years before. I'd made it the night prior, stabbing my fingers a couple dozen times. My house was frenzy of activity, I had a near constant parade of visitors and well-wishers since I'd started making phone calls. Jason, adorably, had not left my side. He'd bonded to my father and reminded me of an orphaned puppy. It was nice to have the help.

The girls came early and all was instantly and forever forgiven. Gene was around almost as much as Jason, taking precious paid days off to be of use and comfort. Kennedy held my hand at the crematorium and took over finding the right pictures to blow up for the display board for the wake. She'd been through this with me before; she was now a veteran. It was only during a toast to my father the night of his passing did she act weird. But she had excellent reason, she was going to have a baby. I cried for the second time that day, tears of absolute joy.

I smiled, remembering that moment. I was going to be an aunt! She'd done an excellent job with the photos, too. I gently traced the edge of my father's high school portrait. So handsome, so manly, his charisma oddly visible in the black and white stillness. I couldn't pause too long. People would be here in 30 minutes and I still needed to set out the food and make a drink station.

\*\*\*

Dad's poker buddies arrived first, setting a loud and celebratory tone to the event. They set up camp on the sofa and told me to change the music. Leeroy loved rockabilly and bluegrass so we cranked it up. Drinks flowed liberally, as did the stories about my father. People poured in and it started to look like an episode of Joelys Jeffries: This is Your Life!

My childhood best friend, Manda, came with her mother who was my mother's best friend. Manda and I grew apart when I discovered boys and she found the Good Word. I forgave her for bible thumpin', but there was no way we could stay close. Manda's mom, Maxine, held me against her huge chest like I was still a child.

James had asked ahead of time if he could come, which I found considerate. I pulled him into what was once our shared bedroom when he arrived. I wanted a private moment with him to grieve in a way only he and I could. My father introduced us. He called him dad and loved him nearly as much as I did. We shared a familiar embrace and cried. I didn't want the kids to see this. To a child, this would look like hope. To us, it was just the intangible ghosts of shared history.

The neighbors from both sides walked in almost together. Robert, the curmudgeon to the right, who constantly cleans his rifle on the front porch. And

Jeremiah, the GILF to the left, who my friends and I like to watch do yard work. I was touched by their thoughtful words. Robert reminded me to keep it quiet after 10PM.

Marcus showed up with some growlers. I searched my phone to see when/if I had invited him. Yup, Drunk-Joe, the night dad died. God damnit, Drunk-Joe.

My father's only living brother was late, delayed by weather. Uncle Teddy was a hybrid of Grizzly Adams and Bill Gates. He'd cashed in early on the tech craze, investing in Nokia with a settlement from an accident and retiring in his 30s. He's managed to invest in every single successful tech stock since, as if he was some wizard time-traveler. His long, gnarly beard was tobacco stained. He lived most of the year in Baja. Their parents were both gone. They also had a little sister who they didn't talk about. I never got the whole story but she was raised by another part of the family when the my grandparents were killed in a car accident. The Jeffries side of my family was almost as tragic as the Mercados.

Several of my father's former co-workers rotated through the crowd. Everywhere I looked I saw memories of hot asphalt and heard dirty jokes. Also in the melee: roaming area musicians he'd worked with and taught. Someone popped in a bootleg live recording of my father's band and I had to hide in my room. I couldn't let people see me fall apart like that. This was, by direct order of the honoree, not a funeral. When I calmed myself, I came back and smiled at the crowded proof of my father's influence and scope in our area.

My cousin Mikey was estranged from his father, Ted. He made a brief appearance with his forgettable wife and generic children. I know that sounds mean, but seriously, they look like models from a K-mart ad - attractive but plain. Plus, Mikey had once held me down and hocked a loogie into my forced open mouth when I was seven. He was on the forever hated list.

Of course, my people were there. My children were enjoying the rare chance to survey a grown-up party and consume unlimited soda. I would randomly grab them and hold them in tight hugs. I felt terrible they'd been exposed to so much death in their short lives. Gene mostly stayed out back, getting Jason and my Uncle Teddy high. He kept the fire-pit raging. The girls were keeping everyone in drinks and the food looking full and pretty. Oakley was monitoring the whole scene, keeping her watchful eye on everyone to prevent disasters.

Pacific Northwesterners, mostly, do not do funerals. We throw wakes, celebrations of life. Knowing I would not have to deliver a formal eulogy was incredibly comforting. I also knew, as a good hostess, I should probably address the crowd and say a few words. I steeled myself with a shot of whiskey.

"Everyone," I started after a deep breath. "I won't take much of your time. My father wouldn't have wanted a big fuss or sad, long speech. We are doing exactly as he asked, a celebration and remembrance of the life and love Leeroy Randall Jeffries: a man that never once shied away from the opportunity of an adventure, the warmth of a friendship, the attention of a pretty woman, or the burn of good whiskey." I paused as the crowd laughed and checked my notes.

"As many of you know, my father was a working musician before I was born. His band, The Drought, was pretty popular around here and had no shortage of paying gigs." Some in the crowd cheered at the mention. "He quit the band to get a 'real job' and provide for his family. If he resented it, he never let me see. My father only showed me love and kindness, and never," I swallowed back some emotion, "never let one day pass without letting me know he loved me. Even if it was unconventional, like calling me a shithead." More laughter. "The year we lost mom would have been his 35th year of marriage. They had their ups and downs but never quit on each other." My gaze, unfortunately, landed on James at that moment. His face was clearly fighting tears. I had to look away. "Theirs was a true and endless love story, an inspiration to any and all it touched."

"So," I started, not wanting to ramble. "Let's raise a glass to Leeroy: a great father, a loving husband, and an exceptional human being. We'll miss you pops." I cheers'd the crowd, and finished my drink. There were a few other speeches and toasts. Most light-hearted, as people shared funny stories about the great man we lost.

As I wrapped up the indoors party, the poker buddies handed me an envelope. I insisted I couldn't accept, but they wouldn't listen. I gasped when I looked, it was easily a couple thousand dollars. They laughed and told me it was only a fraction of what they'd won off dad. I saw them to their cab, and kissed each on the cheek. I'd also received an envelope from Uncle Teddy, but hadn't looked yet. I was abundantly grateful; I hadn't been able to work much and the bills were stacking up. The cremation wiped out my limited savings account.

Eventually my core group, the girls and Kennedy and fucking Marcus joined Gene at the fire. I invited James to come outside but he was taking the kids for a few days. I debated if that was helpful or hurtful and decided to let them go. The grief had me on edge, and I would have hated to unintentionally hurt them.

Bottles and joints were passed around the fire, and everyone told filthy jokes they'd learned from my father. Even Court and Cat, who'd met him once. I was laughing hysterically when I saw a tall figure approaching in the dark. It was Danny, who simply gave me a shrug as explanation, in his hands a bottle and an orchid. I knew why he was there. It was our forever bond - loss.

***

I woke up with a hangover, alone. Good girl, Joe.

And then I heard someone making coffee in the kitchen. Oh, fuck. Bad girl. Very bad girl. Remembering I told a incoherently stoned Jason he could stay on the couch, I relaxed. I still checked for signs of sex. The other side of the bed was still made. All clear.

I laughed to myself, remembering that Marcus and Danny tried waiting each other out at the fire last night, last man standing. I eventually chuckled and told them both to go home. Progress.

***

Well, limited progress.

I slept with another client. 100% not for money, I just got wrapped up in the moment and it happened. His name is John and I'd always giggled at that. John...get it? Anyway, a ridiculously tall man with a handsome, rugged face (no, I don't have a type), I'd liked him right away. He'd been seeing me once or twice a month for over a year. He was the only client I booked during my mourning period, genuinely concerned for his back and knowing he had little to no free time. He always paid generously for the last minute bookings.

He hugged me after he walked into the door. Something about being in his strong arms rendered me emotional and I almost started crying. I had to explain to him why I was such a trainwreck and he engulfed me into his giant frame and stroked my hair. Somehow, the comfort of this man's warmth helped. He was safe. I gathered myself and told him we needed to get to business.

It was a different massage than I usually gave him. Yes, I worked the knots in his back and glutes but when I got to his legs, shoulders, chest: it was loving. My hands were showing affection and it was palpable. As I moved to his thighs, he sat up, took my face into his massive hands, and kissed me. We made our way to my bed and he pulled the simple tube dress off my body. He buried his face in my breasts as he professed how long he'd wanted me. He kissed up my neck and teased my clit with the head of his longing cock. I was melting at the attention, thrilled to feel something other than sad.

That passed quickly when I laced my fingers with his and felt his wedding ring.

\*\*\*

Unable to focus or attend with regularity, I had to take an 'incomplete' for chemistry. I was alright in my psych 202 class, thanks to some extra credit and a forgiving professor. I was grateful I only signed up for 10 credits that quarter. I worried how the incomplete would affect my financial aid, but it was the least of my concerns.

I needed to sell or rent my dad's house, fast. I was able, thanks to dad's friends and brother, to cover the mortgage for a couple months but not much longer. I looked over his loan paperwork and knew that I needed to do some work to the house if I wanted to sell it for any amount of profit. Dad had refinanced about 6 years prior, when mom got sick, stripping out most of the equity. Dad's years of smoking inside had also paid its toll on the home's value. Once again, Jason came to my rescue. Turns out, he's pretty handy. We worked out the same terms: free room and board, smokes and weed in exchange for the painting, new flooring, and other surface updates. One of my clients was a professional carpenter and told me he would do work beyond Jason's capabilities in exchange for massage. Once we could give the place a fresh face, I could easily rent it or look into selling.

My childhood home was in one of the only Portland neighborhoods that had survived the rampant gentrification. Which was awesome in that it was ethnically diverse and affordable, but meant I probably wouldn't profit much in a booming market.

My sleep was incredibly troubled. I was lucky to get a couple hours a night. Starting the day my father died, everywhere I went, even in the soft comfort of my bed, I sometimes heard my mother's voice. My internal monologue was now her slightly accented tone, down to her occasional lisp. And it was every bit as critical as she used to be.

*Sit up straight, Joelys. Shoulders back. You call that a lunch? Eat real food, your ass is big enough. This house is a disaster. You were raised better. Put on some damn panties! What if you get into an accident?!*

Over the weeks her criticisms became near constant. When I signed the paperwork to drop chem? *That's right, Joey, just quit. Like you do everything.*

When I slept with John the john? *Oh, great, you're a whore now. Might as well get paid for it, right?*

When I felt John's ring? *Of course he's married. You couldn't get a man otherwise.*

For the first time, despite the absolute shit-sundae life seemed to serve me, I really thought I was losing it. I didn't know what to do. I worried if I told a therapist, and I was legitimately crazy, they would take Nat away from me. I'd already lost RJ, I couldn't risk it.

I noticed alcohol would calm the voice. I started to understand why my mother drank so much.

\*\*\*

I set up ten appointments for my next kidless weekend, a mix of new clients and regulars. I needed the cash. On top of everything else, Christmas was coming and the Nintendo 3DS my son was dying for is not cheap. I'm sure Natalia's list would be extensive too.

*Oh, yes, justify this lifestyle to yourself. It's for your kids.*

My first was a regular I had great fondness for, Bert. He always overpaid and was so respectful and kind. He wasn't sleazy or pushy. I was always excited to see him and hear about his dogs and his mountain life.

I also saw Adam, my very first client. I wasn't sure if I'd ever see him again. He was an enigma to me. Cute, if a bit short for my tastes. Single. Had a good job. He had good hygiene and seemed pretty sweet. He'd remembered my fondness for ciders and brought me some bottles from a fine independent brewery. Why was this man single?

Later, I saw good ol' Sam. I loved/hated when Sam booked. He's old and on dialysis. His hands shake when they desperately clawed at my hips and ass. I allowed him to touch me out of pity and because I liked the guy. But every time, it made me feel icky. He doesn't smell great - I think that's the smell of sickness. I braced myself for his appointment with one of the ciders Adam brought me.

\*\*\*

Gene had met someone. He's wanted to tell me sooner, but with everything that happened he waited. He wanted me to meet her, the girlfriend, Allie. We agreed to meet at our favorite karaoke spot that coming Friday. I hadn't seen him this excited since he'd switched jobs.

I was not excited. Oh, I'm sure she was great, but I knew what would happen next. He'd get wrapped in that lovely relationship bubble and I'd rarely see him. Dreading the meet-up, I asked Jason if he'd come along as a buffer. He readily agreed, excited to show off his mad singing skills. I was spending more and more time with guy. He wasn't my type, so it wasn't like that. He looked like a bum. He was tall and had a big belly, and a full, unkempt, shockingly orange beard. His hands were fat and meaty, like catcher's mitts. He dressed horribly, sweat pants and worn, holey punk t-shirts. He wore thick, black plastic glasses that never stayed in place and fell down his wide nose.

His laugh was fantastic though. This wildly silly, deep, guffah-huh-huh - completely contagious.

I picked him up Friday night in an uber and we hit Chopsticks. This was my wheelhouse. Karaoke in a shitty Chinese bar and restaurant. The place was already packed when we arrived. Fortunately, Gene had scored us a table. I ordered bbq pork and shots for the table. Mom's voice had been super aggressive all day and I needed some peace.

Allie was fantastic, of course. A heavily tattooed alt/punk girl, she and Jason hit it off instantly. She had a sweet smile and foul mouth. I could see why Gene was so smitten. When we had a moment alone, I gave him my approval. He told me he felt the same about Jason and I reminded him it was only a platonic friendship.

Gene said, "That's a shame. He's in love with you." I was shocked. He'd never so much as flirted. He continued to tell me how they'd talked at the wake and Jason told him everything. Gene assumed my bringing him meant something more. Mom started criticizing Jason's pants and I switched to Long Island iced tea.

When we returned to the table, I started taking long pulls on the stiff drink. Jason asked if maybe I should slow down and I stared him in eye as I finished it in one long suck.

\*\*\*

I woke up in my father's bathtub, my front covered in sick that had been halfway washed off. A rolled towel supported my neck and I had a blanket over me. My head pounding, and feeling like I was going to get sick again, I opened my eyes and searched for options other than my dress. Jason snored on the floor beside me. He'd taken care of me, set me up in a place where I'd be safe, and stayed with me. My mother was also with us.

*Get your shit together, Joelys.*

This time, I completely agreed with her.

**Chapter 13: And Now, Here I Am**

So now, I'm sitting in a circle of 12 or so people in metal folding chairs in a YMCA basement, all staring at me like they'd seen an alien. Had I done it wrong? I thought it would be like I'd seen on TV with a podium and a huge, anonymous group. They asked me to share, so I did. I told them everything from mom's death to last night in the bathtub.

Eventually, the leader, a older man with a ruddy face, snapped out of the trance and thanked me for sharing. I shrug. He tells me I left out one part. I mentally flip through the events: Mom died, divorce, massages, Hank, Scott, making friends, drinking, losing RJ, Marcus, more drinking, Danny, inadvertent prostitution, more drinking, more massages, dad died...what had I left out? Did he know about the threeway? Or the coke?! Oh, god, they heard about the chickens. I am suddenly panicked by all the truth this group already knows.

"You have to admit what you are, Joe." He says softly.

"Puerto Rican?"

The group chuckles. "Let me start," He clears his throat, "My name is Jack and I'm an alcoholic. It's been three hard years since I've had a drink." The group says, in unison, "Hi Jack." and looks back to me.

"But I'm not, like, a total alcoholic." I start. "I've been

having some trouble and I just need some help."
Some people in the group shake their heads. They
don't get it. "No, really. I had a small problem, but I'm
being proactive and taking care of it before I end up
like my mom. SHE was the drunk. Not me." They're
still looking at me with doubt. Not knowing what else I
could say, I crossed my arms and waited.

Eventually, another woman starts talking. "Hi, my
name is Deanna and I'm an alcoholic. I haven't had a
drink in 25 days. I'm so close to my 30 day chip, but
all I can think about is how easy it would be slip again.
I think this will be my fifth time at 30 days. All I can do
is let go and let God, follow the steps, and take it one
day at a time." I close my eyes to fight from rolling
them.

This is not going to work for me.

***

I decide to go to the library to see what kind of self-
help books they had. I'm still paranoid about actual
therapy. I'm an excellent mother, but they wouldn't
care about that. I would be labeled and have to fight it
every day. I carefully read the titles and roll my eyes
again. This is a bad idea. I don't need this
psychobabble bullshit. I just need to focus and heal.
Maybe a juice cleanse. I pick up a few manga titles for
Nat and bolt.

On the way home, I stop at the hippie-juice bar and
overpay for some health in a cup. It tastes like grass
and spinach and a hint of ass, but I feel better
already.

*EIGHT DOLLARS FOR A CUP OF JUICE?! You'll really fall for anything, won't you Joey? Dios, idiota.*

\*\*\*

Now home, I start a check-list. Not my usual list of chores and errands, a list of things I need to fix about me.

 * Drink much less, never to inebriation
 * Fix relationship with RJ
 * Stop using sex inappropriately
 * Stick with juice cleanse
 * Finish school, pick a major
 * Get a good job

There. Done. If I try really hard, every single day, I'll get where I need to be in no time. I seek out my laptop. I feel like pizza for dinner. I need to google if I can eat pizza on a juice cleanse.

\*\*\*

I invited Courtney over for coffee. We were still tense and I care about her so much. I also wanted to apologize to her, if my drinking had caused her any pain. NOT making amends, of course. I wasn't 12-stepping. I was just attacking the problems head-on, and fixing them.

She looks amazing, as always. I don't know how she got so expert in make up but she's flawless. I launch immediately into my apology. She cuts me off and says she's the one who's sorry.

"What on earth for?" I'm puzzled.

"I've been avoiding you." She shrugs and looks down.

"I know. Because I've been a monster. I let Danny -"

"No," She cut me off. "That's not what it's about. That night was incredible. I...I've," She looks down again. "I've been quiet because that night made me realize that I...I like girls."

"Whoa." I softly breathed.

"Yeah." She was equally soft.

"You never thought so before?" I mean, surely she had some idea. We live in Portland. Homoerotic experiences are part of the high school curriculum.

"I had always noticed something felt off with men, sure. But I thought it was just because they weren't, you know, MR. Right. When we -" She blushed. "It felt right for the first time."

"Whoa." I repeat, kinda blown away. I'm not sure what to say or ask. I don't want to push or make a big deal.

"I'm, uh, actually seeing someone. This really great girl from work. I'd felt something for her for awhile and now," She laughs, "I know what."

"That's awesome!" I grin and reach in for a hug. I was so happy for her and so very glad I hadn't messed up our friendship. "Can you believe I went to a damn AA meeting?" I laugh again.

Court did not share my laughter. I look at her, hurt

and quizzical.

"Joe, I love you to bits but you lose so much control when you drink. I've thought about this a lot." She swallows, finding the words. "You didn't get your 20s. You were a mom. And a devoted wife. You didn't get to go out and party and learn your limits. You told me you nursed most of your 20s." She took a breath. "So, now, for the first time, you've got a little freedom and you're living it up -" She must have seen a change in my face, because she quickly adds, "And you so deserve it! But you just haven't quite mastered when to stop." She took a breath.

Thinking about what she'd said, I pause. She was right. I was living my 20s again and going way harder than a mom should. "I'm going to take a break."

"That's an excellent idea!" She gives me her gorgeous smile, with her beauty queen teeth.

"Can we still be friends now that I ruined you for men forever?" She laughs at my joke and playfully throws her napkin at me.

\*\*\*

Nat had started dressing in all black and listening to emo music. When I asked for her Christmas list she asked to get her lip pierced.

Yeah, she was right on time for some sort of acting out. 13-years-old? Check. Divorced parents? Check. Recent death in the family? Check. I gave her space and pretended none of it was a big deal. Mom told me to hit her with my shoe.

That was my mother's answer to everything. She could get her shoe off and in her hand in one smooth motion and her accuracy was scary. Even when she was drunk. Drinking only made her shoe come off faster.

\*\*\*

I don't especially like Christmas. My father worshiped at the altar of Zappa and Hendrix. My mother was vaguely Catholic but only when it suited forgiving her own character flaws or condemning someone else's. Christmas was celebrated with a tree, a few gifts, and some sort of grand, raucous, drunken party I wasn't allowed to attend.

I laugh at a copy of the kids' most recent picture with Santa. Nat's inexperienced hand at eyeliner matches her dour expression and RJ's puffing his chest to prove he's too old for this nonsense. They both flanked the old man, refusing to sit on his lap. I had to result to the 'mom voice' to make them take the picture at all. I guess this'll probably be the last one.

I have portraits from every single Christmas, starting with a 3-month-old Natalia. I guess it's long-held wish fulfillment. I never got to sit on Santa's lap. I remember the last time I asked, and my mother's refusal in rapid-fire half English. She had her reasons: the portraits were too expensive, Santa is for rich white families, why would she give credit to some old guy for the gifts she worked hard to buy me, the line was too long, etc. I remember noticing the line was, yes, long and full of pale-complected families in nice clothes.

I'm mailing out the Christmas cards, trying to write a little personal note in each. One advantage of divorce: my list is now much, much shorter. I tuck a copy of the pic into the card for Uncle Teddy. I had, of course, sent him a thank you card for the check he gave me at the wake, but included more words of gratitude in this one. His generous $5,000 paid for a great deal of the materials needed to fix up the house. I ended the message encouraging him to visit more often and daydreamed about visiting him. I'd been to his beach-side home a couple times with my parents; it's paradise. Maybe I could spread dad's ashes down in Baja. The happiest I'd ever seen him was sitting in the sand, playing his guitar to the audience of the limitless ocean.

I grin at the card I'd received from that sweet client of mine, Bert. It saddened me that I couldn't send one back (he's married). I made a note to thank him profusely. The $100 gift card was almost as kind and generous as his note, thanking me and congratulating me on being such a strong woman. He'd been raised by a single mom and understood my situation all too well.

Looking at the next name on the list, I groan. Not at the obligation, at my own procrastination. Tia Mariana is my only living relative on my mom's side and I always forget to mail her cards early enough to assure they arrive in Puerto Rico on time. She's my grandmother's sister and dutily sends me and the children beautiful cards for every holiday and birthday. We've talked on the phone a few times, recently to inform her of my father's passing. We spoke for a few awkward moments and promised to catch up soon.

Her English is almost perfect, much better than my Spanish. It wasn't a communication barrier; we just have no connection other than the dead.

## Chapter 14: New Year, New Me

I woke with a hangover and a meaty, catcher's mitt of a hand cupping my breast.

*¡Ea' Diantre! What did you do now? This bum?! I swear Joelys, you'll fuck just anyone won't you?*

"Not now, mom." I mutter and Jason moans a soft, "Huh?" into my neck.

"Nothing." I whisper. "Go back to sleep."

I remember starting the evening with a promise to myself that I would only have a couple glasses of champagne. It was New Year's Eve - was I supposed to drink water? I flash over the memories of last night, trying to pinpoint the moment I broke my promise. I just had three, then four, then, oh, there it was: Gene bought everyone a shot. I reciprocated and bought another round and then we all got hammered. Jason saw me home and I pulled him into my bed. I remember he stopped me as it got hot and heavy. He told me he didn't feel right about it with having me this way, being so drunk. I mildly protested and then fell asleep in his arms. I'm grateful he had such a clear head. I sigh in relief at the memory as I gently remove his hand.

I was so happy to put last year behind me. All of the sad and the desperate and the loss would end with

2013. This is going to be my year! Well, after some water and maybe a little more sleep.

*Sure, puta, water will fix everything.*

\*\*\*

Jason stuck around the rest of the day. We'd grown closer, lately, spending a great deal of time together. I thought I'd dispelled any notion he might have had about us, but I guess I may have sent mixed messages last night. We made breakfast together and watched a few episodes of Arrested Development, which he'd seen and I hadn't. I tried to gently bring up my disinterest and he said it was Cohen and Joplin at the Chelsea Hotel. Not understanding the reference, he played me the song Cohen's song Chelsea Hotel #2. I didn't see where it applied until the lyrics, "You told me again you preferred handsome men / But for me you would make an exception".

Jason is kind and smart. He's got an encyclopedic knowledge of music. His laugh makes me grin.

*He's a bum. You want to throw your life away for that? You can jack men off and be his sugar mama. Perfect.*

I apologize, again, for what I did the night before and Jason shrugs it off. He asks if I always act out sexually when I'm drinking and it's my turn to shrug. It doesn't matter. He knows the truth. Insightfully, he says, "It must have been hard growing up with parents that drank like yours. I mean, I really love - loved your dad, but he was kind of an asshole after he had a few."

I laugh. "Nothing compared to my mom. She defined the word 'bitch' when she..." I stopped. I know it's not rational, but I didn't want to finish that with her listening.

"That really sucks." He rubs my back. No one ever offered me this kind of sympathy. Most people only saw the fun, life-of-the-party side of my parents. My father's charm and my mother's humor were undeniable. It was easy to ignore the neglected little girl behind them.

*Neglected?! We gave you everything you could have wanted! You were spoiled!*

"I found a dead chick in our bathroom once." I don't know why, but I really want Jason to know this about me, right now. I've never told anyone. "I was five, and I thought she was just passed out. I pulled her head up on my lap and turned it to the side like I'd seen my dad do before. I stroked her hair and told her it was going to be okay. My mom found us and started screaming. I didn't understand why until I was much older. They made me hide in the closet until all the cops and everyone left. They didn't want social services called. I was so scared. I thought," I start crying. "I thought I did something wrong." Tears falling fast down my face, Jason's paw wipes them away. I waited for mom's thoughts on the memory, but she remained silent.

"Wow." He says softly. "You were only five? You must have been..." He doesn't know what to say. I barely know what to say about it and it was 28 years ago. He pulls me into a big, bear hug and I melt into his arms.

***

Oakley and I decided to join a yoga class for our New Year's resolutions. The only time we could both make work was 5AM on Mondays, Wednesdays, and Fridays. I arrive at our first class on time and ready! New year, new me. 2014-Joe is healthy: physically and mentally.

*In your dreams, mija. This'll last a week, tops.*

***

An hour later, pretty sure I'm legally dead, I lay sprawled on my new, hot pink yoga mat.

*Yoga is for rich, white women who don't work. Your fofo ass don't belong here. Downward dog will come in handy for your 'career' though, puta.*

***

RJ looks at me skeptically. I suppose he has the right; this is completely out of character for me. I give him a grin as I shove the helmet down on my head. Little tight, but it'll work. It's my Wednesday with him and I'm going to make the most of it. He wants more guy-stuff? My ass is sitting in a go-cart, and I'm gonna show him who's boss.

Nat watches from the fence. She's too cool for this now, with her raccoon eyes and My Chemical Romance hoodie. The knows-everything-about-go-carts instructor guy is telling me how to operate the thing, pointing at various parts of the machine. I'm mostly avoiding eye-contact with him because he pointed at the weight restriction when I asked for two rides. FuckHead, I have been driving for 17 years, I know what I'm doing.

I steady my grip, and wait for the kid to drop the flag. I have a plan. I'll beat RJ the first few laps and then get 'stuck' and let him win.

It does not go to plan.

"I've never seen anyone do this before." FuckHead tells me as tries to pull the fencing out of my lap. I'd somehow propelled my cart through the tire barrier and into the fencing. The low front end of the cart flew under under the cheap, temporary chain-link, my body and spent inertia finally stopping the cart. It hurts, but the embarrassment pains me much more. RJ looks so ashamed of me. I can't do anything right with this kid.

\*\*\*

Trying to redeem myself I take the kids to the pizza place with the arcade. I give them each a handful of quarters while we wait for the shitty, dry pizza. I'm sitting alone and feeling awful. I decide to hit the salad bar, because healthy me 2014! Although, I'm not sure my pile of hard-boiled eggs, French corn, and bacon bits slathered in a cup of ranch really count as a salad. Eh, baby steps. In my defense I also placed a whole piece of broccoli on my plate and I'm totally going to eat it.

The place is super run down. It hasn't changed since my parents used to take me as a kid. I think RJ is playing the exact Ms. Pacman machine I used to supply with endless quarters. I yell to him, "I've got next!" thinking, maybe, I could still do something to impress him today. I don't even make it past the second level - killed by Blinky. He wasn't watching anyway.

As the kids attack the pizza, now at our table, I think maybe we do need a get-away. A couple weeks out of routine. I'd never taken them on a vacation, just us three. Maybe I could spirit us away to Baja this summer, roadtrip it and hit Disney on the way back. The wheels spinning, A smile spreads across my face, until mom pipes up:

*You're gonna have to stroke a LOT of dicks, mija. Disney is expensive! Watch out for carpal tunnel.*

\*\*\*

Despite the bruising from my harrowing go-cart accident, I make it to yoga on Friday. Oakley and I agree after that this is NOT for us and hit the diner for biscuits and gravy. We swoop back to my place on the way to grab Nat. Even with her new nothing-matters persona, she's gleeful at the idea of weekday pancakes.

## Chapter 15: Kinda My Thing

I noticed him immediately. He was impossible not to see, broad shoulders and tall, the most handsome, manly face. His face was covered in sexy, dark stubble that was almost to the beard phase and his eyes somehow captured you and bound you to his will. This man was pure alpha, raw sexuality, and purpose.

I didn't mean to ignore my friends. It was the tail end of Oakley's birthday party. I'd kept my self-promise and had two cocktails and switched to soda. Oakley on the other hand, was a mess. We were shushing her every few moments, her voice now a shout.

He pointed to me with his full arm. I'm puzzled. He walks right to me. A direct line, the crowd parts to his will and imposing physique and dominant presence. Now 6 inches from my face, he states as more command than question, "Wanna get out of here?"

"Yes." I exhale. I only realize now I'd been holding my breath since he'd walked in.

In one motion, his arms are around me, picking me up and throwing me on his shoulder. I didn't protest. There was no protest to be had. I want this man. I want him to own me, to be in me and all over me. I need to know every part of his perfect body. I need to know his power on every part of mine.

He literally carried me, fireman style, caveman style, out of the bar and to his truck. Of course he drives a truck. He sets me on my feet by the passenger door and shows some mortality. "You sure you want to do this, baby?" I reply with a deep, passionate kiss. I take his head and short, dark hair in my hands and suck his bottom lip. He takes control of the kiss and bends me backwards. Even my mother's voice is stunned silent.

He opens the door to his truck and I get in, eager to start this ride.

***

He's staying at one of the nicest hotels in Portland. I hadn't been in this lobby since Hank and I'd... I leave that thought unfinished and smile at the handsome man. He's guiding me to the elevator with an arm lightly around my waist. We enter the elevator and before the doors close his tongue is exploring my mouth and his fingers are lightly grazing the outer lips of my wanting pussy. He chuckles into our kiss at the realization that I'm not wearing panties.

"Dangerous," He says, breaking our kiss, but his fingers still exploring, "Wearing that short of a dress with no panties."

"Kinda my thing." I answer, reconnecting with his perfect lips.

The doors open with a ding just as his finger makes it to my clit. We have to quickly assemble ourselves as we notice a small group of people are waiting for our elevator, looking shocked and amused. He picks me up again and carries me to his room. I lose a shoe in the process, like a slutty Cinderella. I giggle in glee at every motion. I can't remember the last time I felt this sexy, this wanted, or this alive.

The room is nice, I'm sure, but I can only focus on him. He tosses me on the bed and removes my remaining shoe. I'm grateful; these heels are sexy but kill my feet. He takes my left foot into his strong hands and starts to rub the arch firmly but with a good amount of pressure. He knows what he's doing. I should know, right?

I never get massages. This might be my heaven. I lean back and let myself enjoy it. I groan in protest when he set my foot down a few minutes later, but he quickly picks up the other and my protest fades into moans and gasps. He tells me how sexy my little noises are.

"Everything about you is sexy. You're raw sex, baby. I knew it the moment I saw you." He says, his voice low and throaty with lust. I detect a drawl; he's from the south, somewhere. He just got hotter. I remain silent, not trusting my voice. His hands move up to my calves. Equally dividing his attention between each leg, masterfully making me feel like he's some 8-armed God of pleasure, he moves further up to where his fingers are, again, gently grazing my womanhood.

By the time he finally spreads my thighs and separates my lips with his tongue, I'm ready to go. One strong lap at my clit and I'm gently shaking all over and my legs tense around his neck. It doesn't stop him; it fuels him into overdrives - manically licking and sucking my delicate bits. I'm overwhelmed, begging him to stop, to slow, but he keeps at it. Moments later I'm shouting and violently shaking.

I snap my thighs together and roll to my side. I need a break after that. I feel a wet spot on the bedding. We made quite the mess, it seems. He lays beside and me and I taste myself on his lips while I tug at his shirt.

*What kind of woman are you? You don't even know his name, puta!*

"Hey," I break the kiss, a bit breathless. "What's your

name?"

"Matthew. Matthew Moore. Yours?"

"Joelys Jeffries." There. Shut the fuck up, mom.

\*\*\*

I'm shaking again after what must be our third or fourth round of athletic, adventurous fucking. He collapses, full body, on top of me. I'm too weak to protest and let his weight hold me, although it hurts and constricts my air. He's a beefy man, his arms thick from either religious gym effort or a rigorous occupation. I trace the lines of his definition and arouse myself again. I roll him off me and climb between his legs. My thick lips and mouth wrap around his spent cock, sucking it back to life.

"Jesus Christ, Joelys Jeffries." He gasps. "Marry me."

I giggle, muffled by the task at hand.

"I'm serious woman. Let's go to Vegas right now. I ain't ever lettin' you go."

The sentiment and the idea of being forever his push me further and I take his whole length into my mouth and throat.

\*\*\*

I wake to my phone ringing. Gene is calling. He never calls, only texts. I didn't think his phone was capable of calling. It must be urgent, so I answer.

"Hello?"

"Jeez, Joe. So, you're alive?" He sounds frustrated.

"Yeah, of course. I'm sorry if I had you worried." I'm talking softly, not wanting to wake Matthew. "I know I -" I laugh, involuntarily at the memory, "I left suddenly last night but I was going to check in."

"Last night?!" Gene exclaims. "Joe, it's Sunday. No one has heard from you since Friday night. You didn't answer our texts. We," His voice breaks, "we called the hospitals and the jail."

Tears well in my eyes. I feel terrible. "Gene, I -"

"No, you don't need to explain. I'm glad you're ok. Please let everyone else know." He hangs up.

Shit. Fuck, shit, fuck-fuck-fuck. What the fuck have I done? I frantically scroll through all the texts and messages from my concerned friends. There's more than 20. How had I managed to not hear any of them? The battery is dangerously low too. I quickly send, "I'm ok and I'm so sorry. Will explain later" to everyone before the screen goes black.

"Was that your boyfriend or husband?" Matthew's drawl enters my desperate silence.

"What? No, just my friend." I reply. "My best friend, and I really upset him. Did you know it's Sunday?"

He barks a laugh. "Really? Wow. Baby-girl, you make time and space disappear. You break the laws of the universe." He's now embracing me. "So, you don't have a man?"

"No. Not even a little bit." I nestle down into his arms.

"You do now." He claims with certainty. I raise an eyebrow at him and say nothing.

"Mine." He says kissing my lips.

"Mine." He kisses my throat.

"Mine." My shoulder.

"Mine, mine, mine." Three kisses for my breast.

"Mine." He continues all over my body.

"Mine."

\*\*\*

I nervously check my list: the chicken is roasting, the potatoes are perfect - being kept warm, the vegetables and sauce, check and check. The cheesecake is uncracked and gorgeous, ready in the fridge. I'll warm the rolls right before everyone sits down. I've got some nice bottles of wine ready and the table set. I rush to my room to tidy my hair and touch-up my lipstick. I need tonight to be perfect.

*Yeah, lipstick will convince everyone that you haven't lost your damn mind.*

I'm introducing my friends to Matthew. Once they meet him, they'll understand and everything will be copesthetic again. The last month has been a total whirlwind of romance and passion. Matthew had just moved to Portland from Texas two nights before we met, a transfer with his employer. I've served as his guide, even helping him pick an epic loft apartment downtown.

The best part? He gets me. He completely understands everything about how I am the way I am and do the things I do. His mom was drunk too. He's strong and dominate but also considerate.

*Considerate? He's buying you, like all the others.*

Shut it, mom.

He's not buying me. When he wants my time, he's considerate of the fact that I should be working and compensates me. He pays for the sitter too, when we need one. I argued at first, of course, refused his money, but there's no telling Matthew "No". Not an option with that man.

*There's a word for men who don't accept 'no' from a woman.*

Answering the knock at the door, I welcome him into my home. He looks devastatingly handsome, dressy casual. A nice sweater under a very expensive-looking leather coat and slacks perfectly tailored to his impressive ass. The cowboy boots are surprisingly subtle, a fine dark leather. It didn't distract from the outfit; the boots completed the look.

"Lemme get a look at you." He commands while gently spinning me around. My freshly dyed pink hair is styled in Shirley Temple curls and I'm wearing my favorite black dress with white polka dots. I feel like a punk Donna Read. "You look amazin' baby-girl." His accent kills me!

"Thanks, handsome." I accept his praise with a grin and a kiss on his cheek.

"How much time do we have?"

"Not much, I told everyone to be here at 7:00." I take his coat.

"Perfect." He says, looking at his watch. I'm being pushed onto my couch, while he kneels between my legs. I know I can't protest, so I slip off my shoes and place my feet on his broad shoulders. This is our routine before any evening out, he likes the smell of me in her beard.

\*\*\*

Courtney and Cat are the last to arrive, together. Cat has some excuse for her fiancee, and we all exchange suppressed smiles. Cat's been engaged for over 5 years. I have doubts. Court swears she's met him, but even she hides a smile. Gene and Allie are snuggled on the couch I defiled 15 minutes ago. Oakley is on some big hunt in Eastern Oregon. Kennedy also declined the invitation. She and Derek had another party to attend for his best friend. The introductions flow and Matthew is gracious and friendly. The roasted chicken's aroma meets the lively conversation and I feel joy and peace. I'm happy. This is my happy.

## Chapter 16: Behave yourself

Waves of nerves spread all over my body, giving me alternating spots of heat and chills. I have never been more unsure about anything in my life. I know I told Matthew I was okay with this and we have a safe-word but I am scared. I'm blindfolded, tied to his bed. I cannot move or see. I know I've been here at least an hour or at least it feels that way. I take a deep breath and try to relax.

I hear them enter. They're talking. I'm wearing a thin, satin slip and I know it's hardly covering me. His friend will immediately see almost all of me. I don't know this friend. I haven't even seen a picture. I feel warm air near my neck. Matthew's familiar drawl coughs out, "You ready?"

I nod. I feel a dick against my cheek and I have no idea who it belongs to. Matthew's voice, much harder now, orders: "Suck it, bitch." I open my mouth and turn toward it, slightly thinner than Matthew's, this must be the friend. Matthew is kneeling on the other side, I now know, and leans over my torso to start licking me. With my legs tied flat, he can't get a good angle - just enough to tease. He sits up and pulls my nightie up above my chest. He asks the other man if he'd ever seen titties so pretty and the man, now aggressively fucking my face, grunts an agreement.

My legs are freed, but roughly pushed up and held firmly in place. Matthew is now aggressively eating me, biting at me. He stops only to tell the stranger to come fuck me. I tense up. Matthew is so possessive of me, how could he like this? Breathe, I remind myself. I feel his weight on me, I feel him enter me.

Matthew moves to the space above my head. He telling me how hot it is, and calling me offensive, harsh names. He chokes me with one hand roughly grabs my tit with the other.

"Yeah, you dirty slut, you like his dick don't you?"

I nod again. I know that's his fantasy. He want me to like it, to love it. I moan as the man started to pump in and out faster. Matthew kisses me and thanks me again. He's over the moon that I agreed to this. For his sake, I try to relax and enjoy it more. He orders me to tell the man to finish in me.

"Blow your load in me. Give me your big load." My word push him over the edge and he starts tensing and pushing hard. This is also Matthew's fantasy. I know want to clean up the mess the man leaves. I can feel his eagerness. I think Matthew is a little bi-sexual, but the Texan in him will never admit it. I man leaves and Matthew gets to work.

\*\*\*

After he was done using me to fulfill his wishes, Matthew cradled me like baby. He carried me to his big bathtub and lathered me and gently washed my hair too. I don't know if he just knew I needed to be cared for like this, or if it was part of the fantasy. He spoiled me all night with sweet kisses and soft, light massages. I'm falling asleep in his embrace, physically and emotionally exhausted. I realize I haven't spoken since the other man was in me, so I lightly thank Matthew for his kindness.

"I would do anything for you Joelys. I would kill for

you. I would die for you. You are my world." His words, in that moment, were neither scary or hyperbolic. This man lives for me and I love it.

\*\*\*

Matthew wanted to take the kids and I out to a Japanese Steakhouse. He'd met them once, in passing. I figured this was a good way for everyone to get to know each other. The kids love the antics of the chefs and going is always a special treat for them. I hadn't told them he was my boyfriend. I was, for once, taking it slow. Well, as slow as I'm capable of going.

*Letting his friend fuck you without a condom is taking it slow? Can't wait to see what commitment looks like to you two.*

Matthew drove us all there in my dad's caddie and told me his first order of business was to buy me a new car. I can't tell if he's joking. He's insanely generous and protective of me. I told him my car was just fine and to keep his eyes on the road. RJ asks Matthew why he sounds like FogHorn LegHorn.

"Well, I say, I say, that's a pee-cule-yar question, young man." Matthew mimicked and the kids laughed. We're off to a good start. When we arrive, I wait for him to open my door as we had this argument once and that was once too often. If he insists it's not a big deal. It's kind of romantic. Nat asks if she has to wait too and I laugh.

We get seated right away at the back grill. There's already another family seated, such typical Portlanders they could be a meme. He's got a sharp haircut but and a full, ragged beard, flannel shirt and expensive boots with no tread. She's racially ambiguous with long, colorful dreads and a baby wrapped around her torso in an Indian fabric. Their well-behaved toddler is wearing a bowtie.

I whisper to Matthew, "Ten bucks says one of them mentions gluten or vegan options while ordering."

"That's a sucker's bet, baby-girl." He whispers back and gives me a quick peck on the cheek. I furtively glance at the kids to see if they were watching. I'm in luck, they're enthralled with the menus.

"Mom, can I have steak this time?" Nat asks. Usually, we're coming here on a budget and I tell the kids we're getting chicken only. Matthew answers for me: "I'm buyin', sky's the limit. Have you tried lobster? Get it with the steak. It's fantastic." I look over him gratefully.

"Oh, really? So I can have sparkling sake?" I tease. I know the answer.

*Sparkling sake and lobster, you're a high class hooker now, aren't you?*

I distract myself by smiling at the woman sitting across the way. I ask her baby's age.

"She's 22 weeks." The woman answers. She's got that blissful glow of a nursing mom. I remember when I used to measure age in weeks.

"I'm gonna put a baby in you." Matthew whispers coarsely into my ear. My blood runs ice cold. I say nothing. I do not look forward to that conversation. Nat breaks my panic asking about scallops. I tell her I was thinking of ordering them and she can try a bite of mine.

Finishing our delicious and fun meal, I ask Matthew if I can at least cover the tip. He tells me I'm cute. He gives the kids 20 bucks and tells them to go next door to the gelato place and get whatever they want. I tell them to behave themselves and we'll be there in a couple minutes.

*What do you know about behaving yourself?*

Sensing something off in Matthew, I place my hand on the back of his neck. He's tense. I ask him what's going on.

"I don't like the way that busboy keeps looking at you." He's not joking. He cracks his knuckles.

*Oh, he wants to watch other men fuck you, but a teenage boy can't glance at your obviously displayed cleavage? That makes sense.*

"Matthew," I start calmly. It's alway Matthew with him, never Matt. He insisted. "We had a lovely night, why ruin it for some kid?"

He exhales. "Yeah, you're right. Fuckin' punk."

"We have to catch up to the kids." I gently start to lead him away from the table.

"I want you to get a large gelato. I want to see if it's possible for your ass to get any bigger." He grabs it discreetly, cupping my cheek. I playfully hit him with my purse.

\*\*\*

Lying in his firm arms later that night (he'd snuck in after Nat and RJ were asleep), he's stroking my hair and whispering sweetness against the top of my head. He's a tamed lion now, the beast of ego calmed and careless. I know only I get to see him in this way.

"I love you, baby." He purrs. It's not the first time he's told me. He'd been saying it since that first weekend, in the hotel. I started believing it a couple weeks ago. I raise and turn my head to meet his eyes.

"Matthew, I love you too." It's my first time telling him. I've felt it for awhile, probably since we'd met. I only now trust myself and us enough to tell him.

"Good. Finally." That sexy accent and bravado return. "So, let's get married already."

"Matthew!" I protest with an eye roll. Not with this again. I know he's not joking, but I can't even think about that yet.

"I'm serious Joelys. I am a man that knows what he wants. I want you as my wife. I want those kids," He gestures toward the kids' rooms, "to be my family. I want you to take my name and maybe we can have another couple kids too. Or just one. I want it all, baby-girl. And it starts with you letting me put a ring on this finger." He finds and kisses my left hand.

I sit up and take a deep breath. "Matthew, my love, it's too soon. And I can't give you all of that." I'm not ready to have this conversation with him.

"What can't you give me?" He sits up too.

Where to start? Another deep breath. "I can't have anymore kids. Medically, can't. Complications from the c-section with RJ." I offer, hoping he'll just shut up.

"Adoption or surrogacy. Is it your egg makers or the oven? Nevermind, I can pay for whatever. We'll buy one. Next." He says decisively.

"Well, I don't believe in taking men's names. I was born Joelys Jeffries and I will die the same."

"Fine. I'll still call you Mrs. Moore in bed, but I don't give a shit if you do it legally. Next."

I'm actually a little stumped. The last name thing had been such a big deal to James. I figured Matthew would throw a tantrum. He's so incredibly macho. Also, the kid thing. I guess I should tell him I'm happy with the number of kids I have. Later. For now, I roll back into his arms and settle the discussion with: "It's too soon. But I will think about it."

*Are you happy? Does this insanity make you happy? What about your poor kids?*

\*\*\*

Kennedy and I met at the trendy boutique baby store to register for her shower. I was so excited to host,

but a little apprehensive it wasn't going to be enough.
I'd planned an impressive menu and few games.
None involving fake poop. Seriously, can we stop with
gross baby shower games? I was hoping we'd grab a
lunch after and have a chance to talk. I really needed
to talk to her about Matthew and I wanted her advice
on my education.

She arrives with the cutest baby bump, highlighted by
her aqua-banded yoga pants. It was K so she was
also wearing a Oasis t-shirt. We squee and awww
over the itty-bitty clothes. I confess to her that
Matthew and I are considering maybe thinking about
having a child together, or looking into the possibility.

"Isn't it a little fast, J?" She's trying to be gentle but
the disapproval screams in her face.

"I know. We're just talking about it. I mean, if it's even
possible."

"How long have you been seeing this guy?" The
gentle fades from her voice and I change the subject.

*She's right, mija. You're acting a fool. Deja la
pendejeria.*

"Which breast pump do you want?" I ask. I know this
is what I'll be buying her. She already has the crib and
most of the big items.

*You'll buy it for her? Don't you mean Matthew will buy
it?*

God, mom, relax. It's not a big deal. Yes, I have his
card. He'd given it to me and told me to use it

whenever. Demanded, actually. It makes him feel good to provide for me. He knows our relationship had been preventing me from work.

As we finish the registry, Kennedy asks about lunch. I make a regret face and tell her I have a class I need to get to. I have a good idea where she stands on Matthew and I don't want to fight.

**Chapter 17: Poking the Bear**

"Hello?" It's time I finally answered this number that had been calling for weeks.

"Yes, hello I am trying to reach Joelys Jeffries. This is Greg Denver with the OCWU." A professional voice greeted me. I had no idea what that acronym meant; I just hope I don't owe them money.

"Yes?" I say tentatively.

"Is this Ms. Jeffries?" He asked without emotion.

"What agency are you with again? And may I ask what this is in regard to?" This is why I don't answer phone numbers I don't know.

"Ma'am, I'm with the Oregon Construction Worker's Union. Your father was a member." Oh, duh! I should have known that. Pops paid his dues for over 30 years, bitching every month.

"Right," I answer. "Is there a problem?" We should be cool with them. They sent a really nice card when dad died. Could he still somehow owe them?

"Ms. Jeffries, we only have 90 days to process this policy or it can get complicated. You're listed as the recipient. I need you in my office as soon as possible." He tone was a bit softer now.

"Policy? I don't understand. His insurance? Does he still owe on his deductible or something?" I hate insurance bullshit. I'm grateful James deals with all this stuff for the kids.

"Ma'am -" He started.

"Please, call me Joe." I hate that ma'am bullshit too.

"Ok," He restarted, "Joe, this is about a life insurance policy. Your father listed you as the only recipient. We have a check for you."

"Oh." My tone was softer too. Dad had never mentioned a life insurance policy. I didn't see anything about it in his paperwork. Of course, that was organized in a shoebox, mostly receipts for medications. I continue: "I guess I need to know where your office is located."

\*\*\*

"To Dad!" We all say in unison lifting cheap plastic cups filled with very expensive whiskey.

I survey the crowd with complete happiness. All my favorite people in one place. Oakley (and the guy she'd been seeing - a quiet but handsome county lineman named Holden), Gene (with Allie, they're now inseparable), Courtney (alone, I guess things didn't work out with the co-worker), Cat (sans 'fiancee', of course), Nat (drinking Dr. Pepper), Kennedy (also drinking soda, also alone, her husband was working), Jason (the weirdness is completely gone, I swear), and my Matthew (whose lap is serving as my chair).

I was carefully holding my hemline on this windy early evening. When I'd tried to stoke the fire, the entirety of the skirt of my dress had swung up, showing my friends and family everything. I should have worn panties today.

"Whatcha gonna do with all the cash?" Oakley asked while she added another log to the firepit. It's the end of March and not yet warm out. She's not being nosey. She's a direct person and I can tell her it's none of her business with no hurt feelings. I shrug.

"We're going on a vacation!" Nat lets slip excitedly. I told the kids right away, of course. I hadn't told them exactly where or when, as I need to make arrangements with James and Uncle Teddy. I smile at the thought of a hot, sunny beach with my kids.

"She's gon' use it as a dowry at our wedding." Matthew joked, wrapping his arms tightly around me. I study Nat's face and see no reaction. I did see Kennedy roll her eyes.

"Maybe she can actually pay me for my labor." Jason threw out there. I grinned at him. I'd already planned on that.

"If it's not too personal," Courtney started, "Do you have to pay taxes on life insurance? I've always wondered."

I knew the answer to this from mom's small policy (which was just enough to pay for her cremation and a little medical debt she left behind). "Nope. I mean, some people do, if it's like, a LOT of money or something. But no, you don't report it as taxable income."

"Man," Gene said, "I can't think of a worse way to earn some money, but really, Joe, you deserve it. This'll really take the pressure off, won't it?"

"Yeah." I said softly, looking into the fire. It wasn't retire and live your dreams kind of money, but it was certainly a big leg up for me. I'd canceled all massage appointments for the foreseeable future. I wouldn't have to accept Matthew's generosity anymore. I could take the time to finish school, or take time to find the right job for me. I can take the kids on a nice vacation. I could buy a brand new car. I'd never owned a brand new car. I won't, but I could. My bank account now $80,000 richer, I had a lot of options.

I'd rather have my dad.

*What about me? Oh, you only miss your father?!*

You haven't really left, mom.

\*\*\*

"I don't know about this Matthew." How often had I said those words?

"Joelys, I swear to you, you will love this. It'll be so hot." He never calls me Joe or Joey. It's always my full name or baby or baby-girl.

"Matthew, I have peed on you. I have let your friends fuck me. I have let strangers fuck me. I let your boss and his wife fuck me. I have pretended to be your sister. I pretended to be a fucking hooker and let you 'buy' me. I have let you tie me up. I have tied you up. I have let you do every depraved sex-act your perverted brain could imagine. This does not look like fun." I hold the giant dildo in front of his face. The leather straps sway into my forearm.

"Baby, pleeeeease?" He holds out the note and then kisses my neck.

"It looks painful." I whine.

"I promise you, it won't hurt." He's set on making this happen.

"OK." I agree with a sigh. "But you have to go to the spoken word thing with me AND you can't make fun of anyone." He nods excitedly as I wrap the leather straps around my hips. The truth is: I wasn't hesitant to do this at all. I've always wondered what it would feel like to have a dick. I'm as excited as he is, slathering lube on his ass.

\*\*\*

RJ scowls at me when I walk into the office. His dad is working out of area today, so when the school nurse called to have him picked up, she was directed to me. The look on his face hurt every part of me. I mean, I'm still his mother. We all want our mommies when we're sick.

*You didn't. Only daddy could make you feel better.*

I sign him out and ask him if he wants me to carry his backpack. He doesn't answer and walks past me to the door. I shrug apologetically at the receptionist.

RJ stands at the front passenger door to dad's caddie. I shake my head no and his pout intensifies. I get in and start the engine. I look back in the mirror to make sure he buckles. I wait. I want him to talk first.

"Why did you wear that to my school?!" He laments after a few beats.

I look down. It wasn't that bad, my deep purple dress. It flows past my knees and the neckline is low, but not obscene. I have a nice, grey cardigan over it, covering my arms and shoulders. This is downright conservative compared to some of my outfits. For fuck's sake, I'm even wearing panties for once.

"I didn't psychically know that 1) you'd be sick or 2) your dad wouldn't be able to get you." I am not letting him shame me. I put up with that garbage from his dad for way too long. "I'm sorry you don't feel well, but you don't get to take it out on me."

RJ flops back in his seat and folds his arms. I wait. This car ain't moving until that kid apologizes. I check my phone and reply to Matthew's text. He's asking me if I would prefer a spring or summer wedding. I text back, "How about spring 2018?" I know his opinion on long engagements, and the thought of 5 year wait will make him go ballistic. What can I say: I like poking the bear.

*In this case, the bear likes the poking, from what I saw.*

Eventually, RJ mutters an apology in my direction. I take what I can get and head out. I ask him if he'd like some chicken soup from the deli and he pitifully nods.

By the time his dad picks him up, RJ and I are in a pretty good place. We ate soup and popsicles and played cribbage. I take advantage of the time to ask him what kind of stuff he'd like to do on our vacation. He wants to drive a Jetski and definitely go to the Mystery House in southern Oregon on the way. He's still bitter that his sister had been once and he hasn't.

Hugging him good-bye and watching him climb into his dad's SUV pulls at my heart. The pain has lessened, but will never stop. My son didn't choose me. He sees me as weird embarrassment, just like James used to. I just have to try as hard as I can to keep a good relationship with him and maybe someday I'll have his respect.

\*\*\*

With the luxury of some money in the bank, I was now only making appointments with clients I liked. Men like Jon Cena Client and blow-job gym guy and John the john. Men who treated me with a great deal of respect and I enjoyed seeing. Matthew was weird about the job. He basically only wanted me to work to support our wild, alternative sex-life. The minute I would talk about needing the money, he'd start in about how he wanted me to quit.

Matthew had been paying all my bills for the last couple months. The money was nominal to him and again, and he didn't take no for an answer. I sometimes worried about Matthew's controlling nature, but he took care of me in ways I had always wished my ex-husband would. For example: driving. When I was with James, whenever we were driving somewhere together we mostly cruised around in my car for gas and parking reasons. Since it was my car, I always drove. Always. I drove us to our honeymoon. With Matthew, he drives or gets us a car service. He jokingly says it's because he thinks women are terrible drivers, but that's his dumb, Texan bravado talking. He simply likes taking care of me.

*Idiota, you claim to be a feminist!*

Dad's house was almost complete. I'm on my way to meet with Jason now, and I know he'll be pretty happy with the fat envelope of cash I have for him. Dave (the contractor/client who'd been helping) said Jason worked his ass off and did 90% of the work. I'm elated to give this to Jason and maybe help him start over.

When I arrived, the 'For Rent' sign was already up in the lawn. I noticed the inquiries were being sent to Jason's cell. I'd have to talk to him about that. He greets me at the door with a grin. Immediately, I notice he's wearing one of my father's shirts and looks great in it.

"Hey!" I shout. "That shirt looks familiar!" I am in no way mad. I carefully went through my parents' possessions and took what I wanted. I told Jason to take or sell or giveaway the rest. The front of the house looks dramatically better. They'd power-washed the siding and repainted the trim.

"I've lost so much weight with all this work." Jason said when I met him at the door and walked in. "I had to start wearing your dad's clothes." The weight loss showed and he looked pretty good. For a bum. I was wowed by the front room. The flooring was shiny and perfect, all new laminate. The walls looked sunny in a fresh, crisp white. He guides me through the house, pointing out all the finished work. I paused briefly in my old bedroom. Memories wash over me and I grin. I continue the tour, happily. This place'll easily rent for $1300-1400 a month, earning me a small monthly income.

"There's more." Jason takes my hand and leads me to the back yard. I see the lawn is perfectly manicured and they even fixed up the siding of and pathway to the old shed. He walks me back there and I see it has a new door too. He opens it and learn it's been transformed. It's a fully finished studio apartment. I'm blown away.

"I used scraps and free or cheap materials from Craigslist." He explains. "You can rent this for another 3 or 4 hundred bucks a month." I look at him speechless. What a fantastic idea.

"But," He continues. "I want you to rent it to me. I can keep an eye on your renters and keep the lawn in order." I smile and he continues. "I need a place to live and I have no rental history. Taking care of my brother was my whole life before I took care of your dad. I have a chance at real job; Dave wants me come work on his crew. I can pay the rent and in a place this cheap, I can buy a car and get some money in the bank." He finally stops. He's so excited and little nervous and it's adorable.

"Or," I hold up the envelope. "You can buy a car now." I put the envelope his hand and he gawks at the bills.

"Can I still rent the shed?" He looks up at me. I notice he's already got one of dad's old guitars on a stand in the corner and some dishes in the tiny kitchenette.

"Of course!" I tell him with a big hug.

\*\*\*

Jason and dad's house squared away, I head home. I can't stop smiling. I'm so happy for him. And even happier that I don't have to really deal with the hassle of renters. Some people are placed in your life exactly when you need them.

Like Gene. I needed a friend and I found the best one I could ever ask for. And when he was ready, he met Allie. Or way back when, in that high school bathroom, crying my eyes out, and Kennedy walked in. Or how Matthew happened to walk into that bar on that one night, and I happened to be there too. I don't believe in any kind of predestination, or fate, but sometimes, it's really hard to deny.

**Chapter 18: Vague Lines of Bullshit**

Nat hands me our big platter to wash. A couple hours ago it was covered in mini-croissant chicken salad sandwiches, which were a big hit - gone in a half hour. All the food seemed well-liked except the jicama sticks in the vegetable platter. White people, am I right? We work on the dishes in silence. She knows I'm upset.

My mind replayed the events of Kennedy's baby shower. It wasn't an outward disaster. I would imagine all the guests went home completely unaware of the subtle drama between the host and the honoree. I asked Nat to take the special chair back into her room. It's a grand, Elizabethan-style upholstered chair my mom had picked up at a yard sale. My dad called it the 'Ugly Chair'. The seat was divisive - people either loved or hated it. Nat had claimed it as her own as a toddler and it lives in her room now. I had attached big blue bows and balloons to it, making Kennedy a special thrown for her big day.

What Kennedy had failed to communicate with me was her grand plan to have a gender reveal at the party. I know for a fact she did not mention this at any point. I knew the concept was pretty trendy right now, the kind of thing K and I used to make fun of. She was pissed the moment she walked in the door and saw all the blue decorations. She managed to keep her rage at whisper, as other guests had already arrived. She silently seethed at the special blue punch I'd made and the adorable blue-frosted mini-cupcakes.

*The punch tasted like ass anyway. And your sandwiches were dry, you put them out too soon.*

We barely spoke at the party. My quiet anger building when I calculated the hours of planning, cooking, preparing, decorating, and coordinating. I made the invitations by hand, in perfect calligraphy. Not to mention the cost, several hundred on supplies and her German-precision tit-sucker. The only smile I got from her the whole afternoon was when she opened the more personal present I'd included: a custom made Beavis and Butthead onesie. When she left, I got a quick, disingenuous hug and an equally impersonal thank you.

\*\*\*

Tia Marianna always telephones at the worst time. I know she's trying to be considerate of the time difference and has no idea what my schedule is like. Her number comes up on my caller ID as I'm about to pull out of the driveway. I'm wearing a sexy teddy under my long coat, en route to Matthew's office to have on-the-clock sex. I put it in park answer.

"Hola Tia Marianna." I answer.

She pauses, maybe confused by the personal greeting. Do they have caller ID in Puerto Rico?

"Hola sobrina. How does the day find you?" She accent is gorgeous and her voice clear despite her age.

"Well," I pause, wanting to keep it simple, "the day is going to be busy so I don't have much time."

"That is fine, I will not be keeping it long." Again, her English is better than my spanish, so you can imagine how dreadful I am at my mother's native tongue. "You know the..." She's searching for the word, "apartment I have on my estate?"

For time's sake I pretend to have knowledge of it.

"The tenants are moving away. I am looking to list on the Air BnB." Ok, Tia's way more tech savvy than I had guessed. "I am wanting to keep it free for you and the childrens to visit. Do you think you could come and visit me? I have items of your grandparents for you. No charge to you, only tourists." She laughs.

I floored by the idea. I need to make a trip to Puerto Rico, some unfinished business, for sure.

*You fucking think? My ashes sit on your damn TV stand for years! Ungrateful -*

"Yes, Tia Marianna, I will visit this summer. I will call you later when I know more details. Thank you so much for your generous offer."

\*\*\*

Gene and I made time to catch the Star Trek revamp. He even showed in his Picard costume, looking handsome in the red shade. I had my comm-badge pinned to my dress. We got some pie after to fully dissect the reimagination by Cap't Lensflair.

Kidfree for the entirety of Spring Break, I head to Matthew's after. I have a piece of pie for him, something to fuel his blood sugar for what would likely be a night of wildly adventurous sex and kink. I knew he was in foul mood, by the way he greeted me wordlessly and stripped all my clothes off. He had me bent over and was angrily fucking me in the entryway to his apartment before I had a chance to catch my breath.

I knew this mood. He just needs to blow off some steam and he'll be fine. I let him have his way, not feeling it. He was pinching my nipples too hard and I never get off from standing doggy-style. It makes my tummy look terrible and I have to tiptoe awkwardly with his height. When it's like this, I don't feel a part of it. I'm just an object, a masturbation aid. Fortunately, it didn't last long.

"Bad day?" I ask him as I try to throw some clothes back on.

"Joelys, I fucking hate it here. Everyone is too sensitive and there's no parking. I miss the sun. Let's move to Texas." I know I have to proceed carefully here. There is absolutely no disparaging of Texas allowed in this home. I try to distract him with the pie.

"Where'd you get it?" He asks, taking the to-go container from my hand and sitting on his large leather couch. I explain where I'd been as I grab him a fork.

"Wait, you saw a movie with Gene?" He asks in a loud, angry voice. "Just Gene? His lil' girlfriend wa'n't there?" Uh-oh, he's dropping consonants. He's going to go full-Texan. I braced myself.

"Jesus Christ, Joelys! A man and woman can'ot be just friends. He wanna fuck you. He's a snake in the grass."

"Matthew, please -"

"Don' you start! Don' you start, now! You know it! You fuckin' slut." The pie is thrown haphazardly onto his coffee table. I wait patiently in my seat. I know this'll blow over as fast as it started, no need to make it worse. He walks into the kitchen and grabs a beer. When the refrigerator doesn't shut correctly, he punches it closed. The stainless appliance now was a big dent in its shiny surface. Angered by the damage, he punches a matching one into the other side.

*This is the man you want to spend your life with? Did you learn anything with the skinny one?*

Too sober to deal with all this, I make my way to his bar-cart and pour four fingers of his decanted 20-year-old scotch. I down it quickly and pour another. By this time, he's behind me kissing my neck. One hand on my breast and one cupping my crotch, he asks: "How does Gene's dick taste?"

\*\*\*

The next morning, I'm wearing a scarf to carefully hide the bruises on my neck and sunglasses to hide my eyes. Make-up couldn't hide the evidence of what that man did to me the night before. We'd enjoyed rough sex in the past, but it was never like this. He took his anger out on my body. And I am making him pay.

It was his suggestion. I would have been happy to be pampered in his tub again, but after he insisted I abuse his credit cards, I gave in. My wardrobe needs up-dating. If I'm still upset after we're done here at the mall, I'll make him take me to the car dealership.

*Yeah, a car will make this all okay, puta.*

We walk past a jewelry store and he escorts me in. I tell him I don't wear diamonds or gemstones, for ethical reasons. He rolls his eyes and asks the attractive saleswoman if they had any conflict-free stones. This being Portland, she's used to the question and shows us a large selection. He tells me to pick anything I want. I see a necklace with a large, sparkling stone set in the bottom-side of a large ring of platinum. It's big, unusual, and gorgeous. I point at it and Matthew helps me take off my scarf to try it on. The girl gasps at the marks on my neck and I give her my trailer-park stare, palpable from behind my sunglasses. She resets her face and tells me it's lovely.

I look into the mirror. A stone this size must be several thousand dollars. I catch Matthew's eye in the mirror. His remorseful face perks up and he nods in approval. I nod back and he hands the girl his card.

Placing my whole hand over the setting and my chest I take a deep breath. I've never owned something like this, something so coveted and worthlessly valuable. I remove my hand to admire it again. It's mine now and I earned it. It's my blood diamond.

\*\*\*

Grateful for the silence, I walk around my home looking for jobs and chores that need doing. I had lied in exchange for this peace and I don't feel guilty. I told Matthew I was getting the kids for a couple days because James had a work emergency. I really needed some alone time. I put all my expensive, new clothes away in my closet and dresser. I left the tags

on because I'd barely tried any of them on. I paused
at the mirror above my desk to peek again at my
necklace. It's really stunning, overshadowing the red
and purple markings also wrapped around my neck.

I grab a bottle of vodka from my freezer. I need to
shut mom up and forget about the night before.

I settle into my couch with a strong vodka-diet Pepsi
and a couple magazines. I have the remote incase I
decide on a movie instead. My phone dings and I
debate if I want to look. I can't remember the last time
I was alone. Responsibility wins, it could be kid-
related, and I look.

Surprise washes over me as I mentally place the
email address. I hadn't seen it in ages. I have an
email from Hank. I finish my drink and pour another
before I open it.

***

Wearing one of my new dresses and my dark purple
hair perfectly styled, I know I look fantastic. I used
special tattoo-covering concealer on my neck and
cheeks, purchased and applied en route. The thrill of
clandestine meetings electrifies my whole body. I
place my whole hand over the necklace in effort to
assess my guilt, but can't find any. It's just dinner with
an old friend.

Hank is perfectly on time and looks almost the same.
Maybe a bit thicker and little more forehead, but the
same distinguished, salt and pepper good-looks. We
embrace at the hostess station and he kisses my
cheek, gushing over how good I look. The

compliments from him, the man I once loved so madly, sends blood to my face. We are seated at a semi-private table quickly.

Even in my new dress, I feel slightly too casual for this place. I'm reminded of how Hank could always make me feel like I belonged, even when I clearly didn't. His affection was the club membership to the elite. It was only in Hank's company did I forget my hand-me-down roots. It's different with Matthew. He's got plenty of money, of course, but his background is a colorful as my own.

Hank and I make small talk and drool over the possibilities on the menu. It's like old times in an instant, planning our order as a team to cover the most desired offerings. He fondly reminisces over how many fantastic restaurants we'd enjoyed together.

"Foodies for life!" I offer him knuckles over the table. He chuckles and shakes his head, as if he'd forgotten my goofy, fun nature. Maybe I have too.

The small talk turns to current events as our martinis arrive. He asks how I am, what am I doing with myself. I smile and take a breath, ready to feed him vague lines of bullshit. But I can't. I can't bring myself to lie to him, despite the fact that I was never honest with him until the night we ended our affair.

"My dad died and I think I'm losing my mind." I start with a bang. "I'm in a relationship with man that might very well be a sociopath and I lost my son." The tears fall with my first blink. "Oh, and my best friend hates me and I," My voice breaks, "I have no idea what I'm doing with my life." I had no idea how long I'd been damming this emotional waterfall, but it just straight up broke into pieces.

Hank hands me his handkerchief (the advantages of keeping older men for company) and signals to our server. He decisively orders a few items for carry-out and asks for two more martinis while we wait. He informs me that we're taking the food back to my place so I can have my melt-down in private. I take a shaky breath and nod.

\*\*\*

Over the rest of the evening I told Hank everything that had happened since we'd parted. I took a shower and put on my sweats. He'd never seen me like this, hair uncared for, without makeup, dressed down. I was his mistress, expected, perhaps by my own standard, to always appear perfect. He looked to take note of my bruises but didn't say anything. He told me I was beautiful without makeup.

We ate the food and hit the vodka. He laughed at my collector's edition Star Trek glasses. How did he not know I was a Trekkie? The night was a perfect mix of old friends connecting and honest discovery. He held me while I drunkenly shared my fears over my mother's new place in my head and told him how I felt immense guilt over not pushing my father to be healthier. I sobbed when I recounted how RJ chose his dad and moved out and the weirdness we've experienced since. My asshole cat allowed Hank to give him two pets before attacking his hand. I saved Matthew for last, unsure how a former lover would want to hear about his successor.

After I told him everything from the first weekend in the hotel to the kink and proposals to the rough sex of the prior night, Hank looked horrified. "Love," He started with familiarity, "this man is not good to you or good for you. You deserve so much better than what he is capable of giving you."

I nod, unsure of what to say. I don't know if I'm ready to give up on Matthew yet.

He waits a few beats, in the way I know he's carefully choosing his words. "Why do you pick relationships have no ending outside of heartache? Don't you think you deserve happiness?"

*Says the man who wanted to keep you as a secret plaything.*

I try to object, but I know he's right. Even my marriage, which had been mostly happy, started preposterously. I was 19 and to his nearly 30; I was uneducated and he had a degree and a career. We were never on equal footing. We never acknowledged that it was only my unexpected pregnancy with Nat that pushed us to marry. Every man since had either a big personality/mental health issue or was a total mismatch or had a wife.

He kissed my forehead and whispered softly, "You deserve love. You deserve so much more than what you have. I regret my part in this. I loved my time with you but I will never forgive myself for treating you so poorly. I'm sorry, Love." I told him, honestly, he had my full forgiveness and we exhaustedly snuggled into a sleeping embrace.

## Chapter 19: Chaos

"What the fuck is this, Joelys?!"

I wake suddenly to Matthew's booming voice in my bedroom. Panic sets immediately and I jump up out of bed and run to him. The fogginess of waking clears in complete terror. I wrap my arms around him and start trying to explain. "I know this looks bad." He grabs my arms pushes me to the ground.

"Who the fuck is this ol' dude?" He doesn't wait for an answer. "I'm gonna fucking kill you." He shouts, pointing angrily at Hank who is reaching for his eye-glasses. He doesn't seem as scared as he should be. He calmly tells Matthew that this is ridiculous and he needs to stop threatening him or he'll call the police. Matthew maniacally laughs. I try to assess the situation. Matthew's large frame is blocking the door. I need to get him over to the other side of the room so Hank can get out.

Hank is still in denial, it seems, slowly sitting up and asking Matthew to calm down. I slowly start to get back up and Matthew kicks me in the side. The pain and the shock of the impact remove my breath and I collapse onto the floor.

"This is too much." Hank says, grabbing his phone. "I'm calling the police."

"No!" I gasp. He can't do that. I cannot have this as public record. I'll lose Nat. Matthew kicks me again, this time his boot connects with my shoulder. He spits on my back.

"I'll deal with ya in a minute, goddamn whore." He returns his attention to Hank, grabbing his arm and pulling him off the bed.

"No!" I scream, lunging at the man's legs. The combination of me wrapping around his legs and Hank pulling away from his grip off-balances Matthew to the floor. I grab Hank in the scuffle and help pull him over the beast's body. I take advantage of Matthew's prone position and sit on his neck. It isn't going to work long, but it'll help get Hank to safety.

"Leave!" I command at the older man. "Go."

"I can't leave you h-" He starts.

"He won't hurt me, Hank. Trust me." Matthew starts grabbing at my ankles. "But he will hurt you. I know you don't understand, but you have to trust me and go. And don't call the cops, please."

"Joe-" He starts again.

"Do you want your wife to read about this in paper?" He pauses at the thought.

"Just go. I will be just fine." Matthew rises under me so lift my legs to put more weight on him. It works, at least for the moment. "I'll text you. I promise." Hesitant, but without other options, Hank walks away. I think about my next move.

"Matthew," I breath in deeply. "I am going to get up and you are not going to go after that man. Do you understand?" I'm speaking to him like a child, but it seems to work. He's tired and moans an 'okay'.

I sit for a bit longer and then slowly get up, but grab the heavy, mirrored tray off my dresser. I'm a fully prepared to take his head off if I need to.

He rights himself, but stays on the floor. I tell Matthew I am going to walk to my desk and text to let Hank know I am safe. Matthew nods, the enormity of what's happened is starting to hit him, I think.

"I'm ok" I text quickly.

He sends me a message in return saying he's up the block a bit, ready to come back or call for help if I need.

"Matthew," I stay calm and even, "This was too far for both of us. You need to leave. Are you ok to drive?" He nods and his face crumbles.

"I can't believe I -" He starts to sob.

"But you did, Matthew. You did what you swore you'd never do. You hurt me. It's over and you need to leave before you get arrested. Now." I firm up my voice and keep the tray at the ready.

"Who was he?" He asks, softly. "Nevermind, I don't care. I really don't. I just want you."

"No, Matthew. You need to go." My voice doesn't shake. I am resolute.

He gets up and my heart races. "Are you sure?" He

asks with a little desperation. I nod, fighting tears.

"I love you Joelys." He says with resignation.

"I love you too, Matthew. Give me the key to my house, go, and never contact me again."

\*\*\*

Hank leaves his car up the road, and sneaks into my house from the back door, just in case. We agree that I should probably spend the night at a hotel, just in case. He helps me pack as my rescue crew arrives. Oakley has picked up Gene and Jason. I hadn't given much direction in my 911 text, except that we needed someone to drive my car and that I needed pain meds.

I make awkward introductions and bid Hank farewell. I want to make a joke about how we need to find a room with a ballsack tub, but it would be lost on this audience.

\*\*\*

"Wow." It's all Oakley can say. "Wow!"

"I know." I nod. Filling her in on the events of the night and morning, it sounds like fiction, even to me and I lived it.

"I'd have killed the son of a bitch." There she is; Oakley has recovered.

*Me too. I'd have castrated that hijo e puta.*

I lean back on the headboard of the hotel bed, adjusting the pillows supporting my arm. I take another bite of the pot cookie Gene gave me. Oakley reaches over and breaks off a piece for herself. She, like me, never imbibes in the cannabis, but we're both a little lost. By the time the boys return from getting my car and checking on my house, we're a giggly mess ordering enough pizza for an frat party.

\*\*\*

Sleep is hard to find, despite all the heavy carbs and THC. Allie picked up Gene but not before he smoked us all silly. Jason is snoring on the second bed and Oakley is passed out next to me, but I just stare at the ceiling. Something had to change. I'd been boy-crazy since I was 13-years-old and it's only brought me pain.

## Chapter 20: Nurse or Teacher

I enter the diner 15 minutes early. I was out of coffee this morning and need some caffeine before James arrives. I down the cup, drinkably-hot by the excess of creamer. I'm halfway done with my second one and the most of the paper when he strolls in. Over two years since I've called this man my own and he still makes my heart race a little. Even after all the garbage we've put each other through, a piece of me will always love him.

Well, some of him.

I have a game plan. 1) James NEVER agrees to something right away. So, I will preface it by telling him I don't need an answer right now, he can get back to me. 2) I'm going to ask for much more than I actually want, so we have bargaining space. 3) I have loads of research for him to look at, which he totally won't read, but it will overwhelm him and make him lean toward my side. Ten years with this man, I have a Ph.D. in Jamesology.

"Heya Joey." He sits with a smile and points at my cup while signalling the server with a nod.

"Heya James." Our greetings haven't really changed over time. I used to call him J-bird, but usually to annoy him. I've a long history of poking bears.

"Thanks for meeting with me. This should be pretty brief." I start.

"Damn," He smiles, "So, no breakfast?"

I smile back. Why was I worried? James is reasonable and we'll work this out.

One hour and two breakfast specials later, we've agreed that I'm taking the kids to Puerto Rico for the month of July. To compensate, he'll get them for good hunk of June and every weekend in August. He says he'll look into custody issues and visas and I remind him the PR is a US territory and they just need ID cards. After a great deal of questioning how we get children ID cards, we agree that getting them passports couldn't hurt in the long run.

As we leave I thank him for being so cool. He laughs at me and says, "Hey, I'm not the one that has to deal with two kids on a nine hour flight." My eyes widen at that reality. I think I'll be looking into buying a couple tablets as well.

\*\*\*

A phone call in the middle of the night is either very bad news or very good news. Never in between. And at 3:30AM on May 19th it was not good news.

Kennedy had gone into labor, two months early. Her mom sounded completely panicked as she told me they weren't able to stop the labor and they are headed to a delivery room. I threw on clothes as I repeated the details of her room and which hospital. I woke Nat and we jumped into the caddie. My hands were shaking and it was only when a stoplight looked blurry did I realize I was crying.

We got there 5 minutes before the little boy was born. 3lbs and 2.5 oz, 16 inches. Kennedy's mom, Iris, came out to alert us of the details. I embraced the woman and congratulated her on becoming a grandma. I asked Nat, handing her my wallet, to go find us coffee and see if the gift shop was open. I didn't want her around for what I'm sure would be the not-so-good news.

Baby-Boy French, to be named, was in the NICU. He's on a respirator and they have concerns about his kidneys and detect maybe a little bit of a heart murmur or malformation. More information to come as they run more tests. I hug Iris again and assure her that he's going to be just fine. She asks if I want to come back and I tell her I have to wait for Nat.

That's half true. I don't even know if Kennedy wants me there. I sit and try to imagine a 3 pound baby, fully half of what my tiny RJ weighed. My thoughts are interrupted by a raucous crowd of obviously drunk men. Derek's friends have arrived. The metalhead I used to bang, Kyle BinTwoStokeJoke, waved and winked. I raise a hand quickly and wish I'd at least run a brush through my hair.

Saintly Nat saves me with coffee. She's got a cocoa for herself as well. She says the gift shop is open. We head that way to get K some flowers. I ask the guys if they got Derek a cigar and some of them sheepishly follow me.

\*\*\*

NICU babies don't get the special viewing window. Preemies are not fun to look at, nor all the equipment it takes to keep them alive. I pace the waiting area, unsure of what to do. I fervently pray to a God I don't believe exists for the health and well-being of my friend's son.

\*\*\*

Iris grabs me and tells me Kennedy is asking for me. I ask Nat if she's cool to stay in the waiting area and she gives me enthusiastic thumb's up. This morning I've learned that my daughter is completely skeeved out by childbirth and I decide I will turn this into a 'teachable moment' when I have a clearer head. I hesitantly enter Kennedy's room and try to steady my face.

That lasts all of three seconds and I am a sobbing mess. She painfully scoots over in the bed and pats the space next to her. I carefully slide in and wrap my arm around her. I congratulate her, hiccuping the words. I tell her that I am so very proud of her and that I know two things for certain: her son is going to be just fine and that she's going to be an excellent mother. She shows me the two photos she has on her phone and we awwww over his adorable face.

We try to keep it quiet; Derek is sleeping on the little couch by the window. I make a joke about how hard he must have worked and we giggle. We share apologies and agree that we were both being dumb. She loudly woots when I tell her Matthew is no longer in my life, stirring her husband. We discuss baby names and I start crying again when she tells me they know the middle name: Joel, after me. She said she had decided that in 10th grade when I told Annie Jackson to go fuck herself after she made fun K's disabled brother.

A nurse pokes her head in and says I've got to go, but can come back later in the morning. I look at Kennedy and she nods. I ask what she wants food-wise when I return and she grins, asking for one my breakfast burritos. I agree to her terms and I give her one last hug and kiss on the forehead. I ask Nurse McRuinstheMoment if I can get a quick peek at my nephew.

\*\*\*

By 11AM, I've taken a quick nap, made breakfast for everyone, dropped Nat off at school (late but she's there), visited and fed the recovering French family, and washed/vacuumed the caddie. Wow, celibacy makes me super productive.

\*\*\*

Jason wants me to come meet his top choice of
people to rent my dad's house. I've picked up some
generic rental agreement forms. We're having a bit of
trouble with the power/water situation, as Jason's little
apartment doesn't have it's own meters, but Jason
says the people he's chosen are pretty chill and
they're gonna work it out together.

We assemble in the bare kitchen and I reminisce over
all the meals I'd eaten in there. My mother was an
excellent cook.

*Thank you! Finally you have something nice to say
about me. Of course, it's about food, fatass.*

I like the family right away. The wife, Erin, has just
retired from the Air Force and is looking to start a
foundation to help female Veterans. The husband,
Cary, looks like Jeffrey Dean Morgan from
Supernatural. Yum. Their 9-year-old daughter is
practicing cartwheels in the backyard. I agree with
Jason; these are the people I want in my parents'
house.

I ask Cary and Erin how they heard about the rental
and I learn they know Jason through the music scene.
Of course the hottest guy I've seen all week is a
musician.

*Married, mija. To a woman that could probably snap
your neck.*

"I actually met your dad once." Cary smiles and
throws in as we're finishing up the paperwork on the

counter.

"My dad?" I ask, a bit thrown. "Where? When?"

"A bar." Jason and I chuckle. "It was about ten years ago."

Before he got sick, I internally reflect. I nod at him to continue.

"I kinda knew who he was; I was a huge fan of The Drought. I bought him a drink and we got to talking. I was freaking out because Erin had just told me she was pregnant. We hadn't been seeing each other very long," Both Erin and Cary smile, "and I didn't know what to do. Your dad was incredibly helpful and I'll never, ever forget what he said."

I can't speak. Mentally I'm trapped in this man's memory of beloved father, once again healthy and bellied up to a bar. I nod for him to, please, go on.

"He told me that," Cary's voice breaks with emotion, "that having a daughter was the best thing he'd ever done with his life." He glanced out the window to his own little girl. "And he was right. It really is." He finishes his thought dreamily. Erin lightly hits his arm and tells him to finish the story.

"Oh, yeah," Cary laughs. "I told him I wasn't sure what to do about Erin, having only known her a couple months. Your dad asked me if she gave good head and when I said yes, he said, 'Marry her'. So I did." We all laugh; that story is the epitome of Leeroy Jeffries.

\*\*\*

At one week old, Declan Joel French was cleared by cardiology, declaring his heart strong and healthy. He'd gained 3 ounces and was oxygenating blood much better. His status was moved from critical to stable and his doctors were very hopeful that, in a little time, he'd be home with his family starting his perfectly healthy life.

\*\*\*

As spring quarter came close to an end, I had to meet with my academic advisor. I'd only taken one 5 credit, on-line class this term. Matthew had financed it, so I didn't have to deal with the rigours and rules of federal financial aid. I'd not met my advisor yet, but a google search showed me a 40ish-year-old woman named Odette, with a background in HR and education.

We exchanged niceties. She called me a returning education student, which I hate. It means old. She asks me what my goals are, in regards to my time at the community college.

"I'm going to 100% honest here:" I sheepishly grin, "I have no idea."

She laughs and tell me that it is alright and fairly normal. She asks if I looked into the school's nursing or teaching programs. What is this, the 1950s? Women can only be nurses or teachers? I know I'm being hyperbolic, but it bothers me. I, of course, don't share my thoughts with Odette D'Underwhelmed. I see she's not wearing a ring and I wonder about her story. Divorced? Spinster? Lady-lover? Her office is garden variety professional and not giving me any clues.

*Stop wasting her time and tell her that you're perfectly happy with a career in prostitution.*

"I was thinking maybe a career as a Speech Therapist when I first signed up for school." I break the silence. "But, I really don't think I have academic fortitude for a master's degree." She gives me a look of pity. She rotates her chair toward a filing cabinet and few moments later has the desired pamphlet.

Chemeketa Community College Speech Language Pathology Assistant Program, I read. Chemeketa is in Salem, OR. An hour and change south of here, when I5 is cooperating.

"It's a small commute, but you can take a lot of it on-line," She starts. She clicks away on keyboard, searching. "Looks like you've knocked out all the pre-reqs, too. You could be an SLPA in under 2 years." I am skimming the pamphlet. It seems like a solid options. I could help people. I wonder what it pays.

"40-50 grand a year to start," She says psychically. "And you can work in the medical end or the education side with the same certification."

I thank the woman for her time, leaving her generic office to ponder my future.

## Chapter 21: You're Stronger Than You Seem

"I want to keep my birthday low-key this year." I tell

Oakley. We're sipping coffees at some tragically hip cafe downtown. On a Sunday morning, waiting for the caffeine to alert us to the fact that we don't belong there. We'd hit it pretty hard last night, Jon Cena client tipping me another tiny baggie of party. He'd come out with me and to meet the girls after we finished. We did shots off his perfect body and later, in the bathroom, I did a line off his hard cock.

*What the hell is wrong with you? Drugs?! You're a mother.*

"Oh, that's just the hangover talking." She dismissed.

"Well, maybe." I sip. "But at the very least, I'd like to do something out of town. Reduce my odds over waking up with Bill Murray." We'd taken to calling Marcus, my Groundhog's Day lover, after the star of the film. She laughed.

"It's such a bummer he's a lousy lay." She doesn't bother trying lower her voice, despite some too-cool millennials shooting us passive aggressive glares. "He's so hot."

"Nice, too. C'est la vie."

"Speaking of hot: Jon Cena client - is he single?" She raises an eyebrow.

"What does it matter? You're not." I grin at her. She can tease, but we both know she's stupidly happy with Holden. The two had recently exchanged keys and 'I love you's. Oakley had the look on a woman hearing wedding bells.

I'll never marry again. Sure, that fantasy was nice with Matthew VonFuckFace. I never really thought we would actually get married. Marriage isn't for me. I gave it the best effort I could and only lasted a decade. I honestly don't think I'll have a serious relationship for long while either. Fucking randoms is way more fun and way less complicated.

"Earth to Joe." Oakley waves her hand at me. I guess I zoned out for a moment.

"Sorry, I was thinking about Jon Cena client's abs."

\*\*\*

Tia Marianna and I were now communicating a couple times a week. I'd grown fond of hearing from her. I learned we both like to organize things into the smallest details. I also learned that I have some second cousins in the area and some other distant family. I looked forward meeting these people.

I've never felt like I belonged here. I'm too dark to be white, too light to be latina. My ass has never fit in jeans. I'm always told to shush and settle down. I wonder if in Rincon, Puerto Rico, surrounded by people who, at least partially, share my DNA, maybe, I'll feel more at peace. Or I'm too Americanized and I'll be awkward and homesick the whole time. Doesn't matter, the tickets are booked and we're headed out on the 2nd of July.

\*\*\*

Swimsuit shopping for our trip, Nat and I decide not to look in the mirrors at all and just rely on what feels good. I've tried to raise the girl to think her body's perfect, exactly as it is. Of course, unless you keep them in a bubble - young girls have constant pressure to look a certain way. When she refuses our traditional CinnaBon that concludes every trip to the mall, I worry she looked in the mirror.

I know I did.

On the way to the parking complex, I ask her if we forgot anything. She checks my meticulous list and says, "Duh, trunks for RJ." Oh, to be a boy and not have to try on anything. He's a boys' medium in every store. We turn around to hit the large discount department store behind us. I catch her eying the tattoo/piercing grotto next to it.

"Wanna poke your head in there while I grab them?" I ask.

"Come with me." Despite the eyeliner and band tee's, she's still my shy, anxious child. She couldn't order for herself at a restaurant until she was 9-years-old.

However, a daughter that wants my company is something I will never refuse. We walk in and ooh and aww the ink art on the walls. The artist that works here has some talent. His shading is superior - at least on paper. I briefly considered trying to become an tattoo artist. Half the work is lettering, which is my forever passion. I have incredibly steady hands. But, I don't love it in the way an artist should. I think it's cool, just not for me.

"Mom?" She's nervous again.

"No, you can't get a tattoo." We laugh.

"Can I get an industrial?" I know that's in the ear, but I forget where. I shoot her a quizzical look and she she points at a bar across the top of the ear on a detailed mannequin they have on display.

"Absolutely." I say instantly to her surprise. I honestly thought she was going to ask for a nose or eyebrow ring. I mean, come on, it's just her ear. It'll heal if she hates it.

I get the attention of the bored cashier and start mentally practicing how I'll sell this on her dad. I see there's a buy-one-get-one special, second piercing half off. Not one to turn down a good deal, I ask for an industrial for my daughter and a tiny stud in my right nostril. Why not? I've always wanted one and if I hate it, it'll eventually heal.

All things heal in time.

\*\*\*

The next morning, Nat and I show off our new face holes and their jewelry to Kennedy. We're going to drive her to the hospital so she spend the day with little Declan. She's not cleared to drive quite yet and Derek's at work. I've yet to hold the kid, but it should be soon.

She's not ready to go and I ask how I can help. She nervously looks around, bewildered. I know this part of K. She's a perfectionist and when she's in a situation beyond her control she gets overwhelmed. I tell her to go do her hair and makeup, while Nat and I pick up the house. It's not messy, but I know the two dishes in the sink and the unmade bed will bother her all day.

I ask to see the nursery first. I want to help her picture a healthy son in the room. I ask her simple questions about the space. I stand over by a bare wall and tell her it needs something. She grins, knowing I have an idea.

"Trust me?" I ask.

"Almost every day since freshman year."

\*\*\*

After delivering Kennedy and getting a quick look at Declan, I drop off Nat and get a white mocha. I hit the hardware store for paint and brushes. I have loads of paint brushes, but I don't want to muddy them with latex wall paint. Rather, I don't want to clean it off. I'll just toss these cheap ones when I'm done. I also get a floor guard, some trays, a yard stick, and head to the check out. But first, I detour to the fencing supplies where I'd seen an extraordinarily good-looking man heading.

I catch up with him and make eye contact. He smiles. I look for a ring and get an all-clear.

*Like that's stopped you before!*

"I don't have much time." I start. "Here's my number," I hand him my card, "use it if you'd like to get a drink or something."

He's stunned as I walk away, and then composes himself enough to ask if it's my cell listed. I had the cards made up to semi-legitimize my massage service. It only has my email, cell, and first name under the 'Massage Therapist' in embossed script. I toss a nod and wink back to him and walk around the corner.

He's texted me before I get my car loaded.

\*\*\*

After hours of work, I step back to admire what I have done. I snap a couple pictures while there's good lighting. In antique typewriter style lettering, I've carefully painted the famous Winnie-the-Pooh quote: "You are braver than you believe, stronger than you seem, and smarter than you think". It's simple but unique, slightly off-centered on the wall. To the farther right, I've painted the backs of Pooh and Piglet walking hand-in-hand down a leafy path with a row of autumn trees fading into the corner of the room. I'm rusty but these characters are so simple it was easy. It looks perfect. I know Kennedy will love this. The crib's bedding is all Pooh themed and she'd written the same quote on my facebook wall countless times.

I check my phone and hustle to clean up. I know K and Derek won't be home to see this until 8pm or so, but I'm meeting the Hardware Hottie for drinks in 45 minutes.

\*\*\*

The girls are making fun of me for my checklist as we

pack Oakley's SUV for my birthday get-away. I get it; it's asinine. The list had already gotten me in trouble that morning when Nat glanced at it. She's reading the items off, and gets to 'shave pussy'. She looks at me, incredulous.

"Why? Why would you shave that?!" She's 13 and thankfully pretty sheltered.

"Swimsuits." It's all I got. "To make sure the hair doesn't show in the side of my swimsuit. I have a lot down there - I'm Puerto Rican."

"Will I?" She looks horrified.

"No, mija, you got your dad's generic European genes." I say and then smoothly divert the subject, asking her if she's packed to go to his house.

I relate the story to the girls and they laugh hysterically. Everyone but Oakley has pre-gamed a little with some good ol' B&J's wine coolers. Fuzzy navel. I joke that it tastes like high school blow jobs to me and we share more laughter. We're headed to a condo on the coast I'd found to rent for super cheap. It's a one bedroom, but the main area has another murphy bed and a fold out couch. Three beds and four girls, we'll make that work. The cramped quarters are worth the beachfront location and the hot tub.

*Maybe you and the lesbian can share a bed. Again.*

It's early June so the beach isn't all that warm yet, not this far north. However, it's breathtakingly gorgeous. We're driving to a little town named Lincoln City. I know it well, most of my family vacations had been spent there with James and the kids. I tell the girls about a kite shop where we can rent giant performance kites in the shapes of dragons and whales. They're unimpressed; I think they were hoping for a less wholesome weekend.

Cat's pretty upset over a fight she'd had with her imaginary fiancee. I ask her why they hadn't set a date. She has a bunch of excuses, mostly financial. I tell her eloping is pretty cheap. We all started talking about where we'd elope to, were we in the position. Court asks about my wedding. I laugh.

"Four months pregnant at the courthouse and lunch at Subway with my parents after." Everyone giggles. "Can't resist those $5 foot-longs!"

"Speaking of foot-longs," Oakley starts with a smirk, "Did you tell them about the Hardware Hottie?" Whoops and hollers fill the car; Court and Cat demand details.

"Well, I'm never one to kiss and tell," I lie, "but, there is such a thing as too big. I mean, it took 3 days for my cervix to recover." Our laughs and raunchy jokes weave into the highway's rhythmic noises the rest of the car ride. My 33rd year is off to an excellent start.

\*\*\*

That night, drunk, I sit at someone's sandy bonfire, dreamily staring into the flames and the endless ocean beyond them; contemplating the why and how of it all. Oakley has won the crowd's affection with her guitar, Court joining in on the harmonies. I love my friends, my family by choice. My meditation is broken by a cute, younger guy asking if I'd like a drink. I look down at my half-full plastic cup, pound it, and say, "Yes, please."

After a few pleasantries, I'm making out with him. He said he was a good-kisser and I told him to prove it. He wasn't wrong. I tell him we should go back to my room so I can sit on his face. He accepts my offer and I quickly text the girls that I'll be back soon.

\*\*\*

The next night, the girls and I get pretty and head to the little tavern up the shore. I've promised Oakley a mechanical bull and Cat $2 well drinks. Court is gleeful to discover they have karaoke. Cat and I settle up to the bar. I study her pretty face and kind eyes.

"You should marry that boy." I tell her out of nowhere.

She's perplexed. "How could you, of all people, say that? You hate marriage!"

I carefully think about my next words. "Do you like olives?" I point at the bartender's garnish station.

"You know I do!" She laughs. She'd had a can of the briney balls of hate for breakfast.

"I fucking hate them."

"I know!" She laughs. She'd teased me all morning over the way I'd gagged over her meal choice.

"Everyone is different. Some people like olives. Rational, intelligent people do not." I wink at her. "Some people are meant to get married and love it. Some people, like my mom and dad, have marriages that give them strength and meaning. But some people never marry at all and love their lives too. I'll tell you one thing about my marriage." I pause. I have so much I want to tell her but I also want to keep this night fun and light.

"My divorce was the worst thing that ever happened to me. It was worse than losing my parents. It emotionally eviscerated me. And if I had a time machine and could go back and never even meet James, I wouldn't do it. Not for my kids' sake. For my own. Knowing everything I know now, I'd still marry him. Despite all the resentment and ugly, I am the person I am today because of what we had. I'm grateful for the time we had. Ours wasn't a lifetime kind of love but that doesn't take away its greatness." I take a quick breath.

"Marry that boy. Even if you become a statistic, it'll be worth it. You'll be a part of something wonderful and profound and you, my lovely friend, deserve that."

"Whoa." She breathes out.

"Yeah, we needs shots. And don't tell anyone I said all that."

We pound three rounds of tequila shots and turn to study the crowd. I see the BonFireCasanova over on the deck. I ask Cat if I should go for the sequel or find some strange. She just laughs, staring at her phone. I peek and she's sending a loving text to her man. I kiss her on the cheek and run off to catch Oakley's turn on the bull.

\*\*\*

When we return from the beach I have the beginning of a tan and a million things to do to prepare for the month in PR. The kids would be spending most of their time before we leave with James and a week with his mom up in Seattle. I was grateful for the break, I needed to work. I knew I had a bunch of cash in the bank, but I want to try to cover as much of this trip as I can by myself.

*You need to get a real job, you lazy piece of shit. This is not work.*

Reminiscent of my very first weekend as a rub-and-tug provider, I got a cheap room and placed ads on craigslist and backpage. In the five days and nights I worked, I saw countless men and one couple. The couple, an middle-aged man and woman, had done this before so I pretended that I had too. I rubbed him first while she watched from the bed. When it came to his 'happy ending', I invited her to come closer. He grabbed her tit roughly and came in 20 seconds. I was nervous about her's, but after all the thigh rubbing and teasing she was ready. I couple minutes of even, steady pressure in a circular motion around her swollen clit and she was panting out an orgasm. It was pretty fun and an easy $300.

A regular that I adored, Bert, met with me after the couple left. He's so incredibly respectful and considerate. I gushed over the thoughtful birthday card and gift he'd sent. I offered him a discount, but he refuses to pay me any less than $150. Just as he's cumming, his hand lightly grazes my knee in the tamest of gestures. It's sweeter than it is sexy, almost comforting to both of us. When he leaves, I give him a peck on the cheek.

*Awww, I'm sure his wife would find this all very heartwarming.*

Mom's ever-present during my work week, of course. It's a little easier to tune her out, these days, but I still constantly wonder if she'll ever leave. Man after man, I worked tirelessly, almost to prove something. Since I started this job, I've had to constantly remind myself that I was not being exploited. It's minimum wage earners that are exploited. It's sex workers with pimps that are exploited. It's people who trade their health and safety for money (oil workers, coal workers, commercial fishermen) that are exploited. I am empowered. I am goddess of sexual energy providing needed and wanted service.

Ok, maybe that's a bit much. But I did earn a little over $4300 in five days. And $2400 more when I set up shop for three days the next week.

**Chapter 22: Land of the Free***

We've got 40 more minutes until boarding at Newark Int'l airport. I'm already frazzled and the kids are done. We stopped in Denver, spending our 2 hour layover looking at all the murals. The flight to Aguadilla, PR is another four hours or so, and then we've got a spendy taxi booked to get us to Rincon. RJ is already tired of his new tablet and grumpy. I see if the possibility of food can lift his spirits. I tell him he can pick whatever he wants from the large food court.

"Pizza Hut?" It perks him a little. I nod and give Nat a $50 to feed herself and her brother. I head to the Starbucks across the walkway. We had to check our bags, which initially I lamented but now feel gratitude. It's one less thing to lug around now.

Waiting in line I turn to check on the kids. I look around the coffee kiosk. The last time I was in one of these, I rage-quit my stint as the world's worst barista. I hear someone call my name and turn around, perplexed. Standing in line, two behind me, is Hank. I hadn't seen him since that fateful morning with FuckFace.

"Well, of all the gin-joints…" I say incredulously as I walk back to him. We embrace tightly.

"What in the world are you doing here?" We ask at the same time. I burst into giggles. I explain the trip and point out the kids, now sitting and waiting for their food. Nat blows the paper straw cover from her soda at her brother. He laughs at the scene and informs me that he's enroute to Berlin for a conference.

"Wanna trade?" I offer. It's our turn to order and Hank offers a card to smoothly pay for mine as well.

"If you're buying, I'll have lemon loaf too." I wink at him. I invite him to join the kids and I, thinking he'd decline but a few minutes later I'm seated with my kids and my former, married, older lover. Nope, not awkward, at all.

I introduce him as an old friend. They accept it, not

knowing any reason to suspect otherwise. I ask what they ordered just as the number is called. They sit the trays down and I see: two personal pizzas, breadsticks, wings, and some giant cookie thing. I laugh and ask Nat if there was any change. She shrugs, and I don't press it. We're on vacation. I grab a wing, and offer the bounty to Hank. He looks suspicious and I wonder if he's ever actually eaten anything from Pizza Hut. He graciously breaks a piece off a breadstick and takes a bite. His strong Canadian sensibilities only allow him to nod slightly and say, "Interesting."

I try not to overthink his being here, today. There's no fate, no kismet. We're not star-crossed lovers. This is not a sign from the universe. If I'd kept on as his mistress, I'd possibly be headed to Berlin today. Maybe I'd have a daringly modern apartment in LA and, I don't know, a job in set design. Maybe I'd be happy in love with a smart, charming man that treated me well.

As well as a married man can, that is. I can't glamorize what we had. He was selfish and I was thoughtless and it's over. I even got an apology from him, something I didn't know I needed. What we could have had would have been a lie. I would have lived in the shadows, in his shadow. I would have been a pet. I may have spent the better part of the last two weeks stroking dicks for cash, but at least I was free.

\*\*\*

The cabbie spoke so fast I couldn't keep up. My Spanish sucks; it's time for me to admit. It's late and the kids and I are wiped out. According to google the route is only 35 minutes, but we've easily been in this cab for an hour. My body is achy and my stomach sick from travel and crappy food. I need a soft bed and a ton of water.

We finally arrive to a loud, well-lit party in front of Tia's house. I pay the driver, chuckling at the memory of Nat freaking out that we didn't convert our money. I patiently said for the hundredth time, "Puerto Rico is in America! Well, kinda." He thanks me and helps with the bags. Tia Marianna runs out to meet us.

She's spry for her 70-plus years. He long silver hair is gorgeously braided to the side and she's wearing a short, colorful dress. I hope I look half this cool at her age. She grabs in me a firm, loving hug, crying, "Joelys, Joelys!! You have come to home, finally!" I'm so overwhelmed with the affection, I barely notice how she says my name: YO-leese, Yo-leese. I'd never thought about how my name, my own name, would be pronounced here. She makes me feel like a soldier returning from war. After she's done with me, she turns her attention to the kids.

"Too skinny!" She smiles at me. "Do they eat?" She turns Nat for inspection, just slightly, examining her face. "Gorgeous!" She hugs my daughter. "Natalia! As beautiful as the whole ocean!" Nat blushes.

"And this young man? Not Rafeal! I was told little Rafeal was a young boy!" Her kidding makes RJ forget he hates being called Rafeal. She hugs him tight and he accepts her love.

We're invited to the come and meet everyone. She

announces all the crowd, one by one, but there's no remembering the names or the relationships. I hear cousin a lot and a few nephew/niece mentions. I have no idea how these people are my kin. I genuinely thought Tia was all I had left and she never had children. People are grabbing at me pulling me into a bunch of conversations. It's a little much for me. I ask to use the restroom.

Splashing my face with cold water helps. It's humid here in a way I've not experienced. And crowded. I grew up with a mom and a dad and that was it. We were small but close. I reminded myself that I may be slightly uncomfortable now, but it was to better understand my heritage, what maybe makes me the person I am. I glimpse out the window and see water in the moonlight.

After hours of food and music and answering questions about our lives in 'the states', we're finally shown to the guest-house. Our home for the next month, it's ineffably charming. The rattan doors swing out to a small shoreside deck. The bed is made with all white linens. The bathroom and kitchen are small and functional. It's the walls, bamboo or something equally tropical, where I understand the magic of this tiny home. I'm instantly and madly in love. The walls have fantastic hand carvings everywhere. There's a subtle, anaglyphic depiction of the Last Supper in the kitchen and tropical flowers in the bathroom. I let my hand follow the smooth raises and valleys of the artisan work, entranced.

I set RJ up on the couch and he's snoring before I turn out the light. I leave the swinging doors open so we can hear the waves. Nat and I fall into the bed and finally put this long, exciting day to rest.

\*\*\*

Waking from the most peaceful, deep sleep I've had in years, I raise slowly. I don't want to disturb Nat. She's slobbering all over the pristine white pillowcase. I ease into the restroom and relieve my hurting bladder. I do some self inventory: slightly achy, need coffee, feeling the beginning of some cramps in my legs. I look in the mirror and I don't look nearly as rough as I feel. The humidity has a weird, curling effect on my hair. I look wanton and somehow younger. This is my new favorite mirror on Earth.

I throw on a little chapstick and a cute, strappy dress. I immediately find Tia Marianna sitting on her porch with what looks to be a coffee pot. Bless this woman.

"Buenos días, Tia!" I grin at her. She looks amazing in a long, silky slip and her hair gracefully piled atop her head.

"Ahhh, good morning, me bonita! Café?"

"Oh, God, yes please." I sit in the chair next to her.

She pours the cream in first and then laughs and says it's probably too much. I grin and tell her it's perfect. I peruse the landscape and tell her everything is absolutely perfecto.

\*\*\*

I don't plan much for our first day. We've got to adjust to the new time zone and we're still tired from all the travel. Also, we don't need plans. My aunt's house, which I learned last night was my grandparent's home, is on the freaking beach! She's 15ft from the shore of a gorgeous inlet. It's shockingly white sand and and turquoise water are private to just her and couple other houses.

The four of us laze about on the hot sand, occasionally rising to cool off in the water. The kids are slathered in SPF90, but I still send them in to get a break from the sun at mid-day. They're super white; they have to ease into this world. We all have plenty of plantains to try to combat the cramps and for lunch Tia makes us ham sandwiches with a delicious lime mayo and avocados. We nap until dinner and eat her amazing black bean soup, frijoles negros, and gorge ourselves on these weird, sweet rolls. I beg her to teach me how to make them and she winks, promising to teach me a great deal this month.

\*\*\*

Tia's plan was to take us into town today, our second day here, but it's the fourth and a federal holiday so she wants to avoid the crowds. She advises we'd all be happier if we just stay on the property and have a repeat of the day before.

RJ's a bit disappointed (I'd promised to find him snorkeling equipment) but it's assuaged the moment he learns the neighbors also have a 10-year-old boy and the two become fast friends. I'd already googled for places with public displays of fireworks and learned that, as a whole, Puerto Ricans aren't too enthusiastic about Independence Day. The mystery of the homeland deepened. I had a lot of questions.

Sipping our too-creamy coffee, I ask my aunt: "Do you consider yourself an American or Puerto Rican?"

"I Puerto Rican." She says proudly and sits up slightly.

"But Puerto Rico is an American territory. You fly our flag. You use our currency. You have the rights of an American Citizen." I realized I was sounding pretty nationalist, so I softened. "Why do you feel that way?"

She waits a moment, perhaps choosing her words. "You have a house with...tenants. Four people who share the rent. You understand?" I nod. "Everyone pays. The house needs painting, yes? Everyone buys in on the paint. But you do not get the…" She's looking for the word, "choice, si, choice. You do not choice the paint because you live in the basement."

What a fantastic analogy. This woman is brilliant. Taxation without representation makes people throw tea into harbours. I wouldn't want to light a bunch of fireworks either.

\*\*\*

Writing out my first set of postcards (picked up at the Airport in Aguadilla), I send missives to Gene, Kennedy, Oakey, Court, Cat, and Jason. I to find the words to describe the beach I'm currently sitting upon. There's hardly any room to expand or get into much detail. I want to bring them all here someday. I wrap it up; I've got to get dressed. The family is coming over again. This time, I'm going to take notes.

## Chapter 23: History Lessons

RJ jumps on my bed, excited to start the day. I'm less than thrilled. Last night, my Tio Paulo (I think?) invited me to sample what he claimed to be Puerto Rico's finest rum. The older men were all sitting a table playing a drinking game involving cards and counting. I asked to play and it turns out: I'm really bad at it. Or really good. It doesn't matter; I got hammered.

We have plans to go into town and do some shopping and take surfing lessons. Rincon is a surfer's destination and hosts many surf events and competitions. I'm hoping to look into renting a car as well. I don't want to be an inconvenience to Tia Marianna. I tell RJ that mommy needs coffee, a shower, and at least an hour of quiet or we're not going anywhere. He runs off and a few moments later, Nat appears with a steaming mug.

"Tia Abuela said you'd need this."

After I right myself, hydrate, and make sure everyone is ready, we take off. I'm surprised by Tia's choice of vehicle: a rugged, military style Jeep. As we drive, I see a few more of these kinds of rigs out on the roads. Her house isn't far from our first destination. We arrive a few minutes later at a huge open market, almost a full city block. There's a mix-match of booths and tables and little tents.

We luck out and find parking close to the action. When RJ runs toward a display of beautifully painted surfboards, he's nearly hit by a large, orangish fish. A man is throwing them from a cooler to another man in a booth. I giggle and tell Nat that this is better than Pike's Place in Seattle. I yell after RJ to stay close. Tia is headed the other way to one of the many produce vendors.

I learn that we're here at the golden time. Late enough that vendors will start to lower prices and haggle, but not so late that the selection is poor. She clucks at a man selling big packages of socks and t-shirts, and whispers that they're paper thin and fall apart in a day. I see an artist sketching folks and ask Nat if she'd be willing to sit for one. She agrees and we head that way, leaving Tia to chat with some old ladies sitting under an umbrella.

"¿Habla Inglés?" I ask the man sitting at an easel, head buried in a sketchbook. He does not look up.

"No sé, ¿hablas español?" He tosses back.

"¿Cuánto para elllll, uh, arte?" I ask.

"Fine." He sighs in perfect English. "We'll do it your way." He looks up and I almost gasp. This man is gorgeous. Caramel skin, contoured cheeks, and a strong jaw frame his large, dark eyes. His hair skims his brow and he has a stark, perfect goatee. He's wearing an old, beaten dress shirt with the sleeves rolled up and the front opened enough to reveal his lean, strong body.

"It's 20 for a drawing of one person, 40 for the both of you. You'll have to sit for around a half an hour." He's impatient, restless.

"Oh, just her." I wrap my arm around Nat.

"Ok." He points at the chair across from him. "Sit."

I leave my daughter with the brooding artist to find RJ.

When I return, I see his work and it's amazing. He's captured my daughter in a way I thought only I see. It's the eyes, I decide. He's somehow, with just charcoal, managed to show them bright with intelligence. He perfectly shaded the cleft of her chin, without cartooning her. There's a subtle brilliance to his work, no superfluous lines, every stroke and shade deliberate to tell the story. I'm beyond pleased.

As I admire the drawing, Tia Marianna joins me. She also praises the work. I'm floored by the man's talent and wonder why he's wasting it here, for $20 a pop.

"He works here to study people. He likes the variety." Was my aunt some sort of enchantress? How did she know what I was thinking? "I've known him since he was a boy." She says proudly. "Aye, Xavier!" She calls out to him. He glances up quickly from his work, grins, and returns. A few moments later, he's signing it and ripping the sheet carefully from his large pad.

I take it from him, delicately, in total awe. Nat comes over to look and she's stunned speechless as well. I thank the man and grab some cash for him. He takes it and gestures for me to sit.

"Oh, no, no. I just wanted a portrait of my daughter. I'd get one of my son too, if he could sit still for more than 5 minutes."

"Please. I'd like to draw you." He says calmly but

there's an urgency in his eyes.

"I really can't. My son, see over there?" I point at the impish child, wildly gesturing us to leave. "He's eager to get to a surfing lesson I promised. Maybe some other time?"

"They are to be staying at my home, Xavier. You come to dinner, soon?" Tia asks the man. He accepts and they kiss each other's cheeks. As we leave, I take one last look at the handsome man and he hasn't stopped watching me.

"Is he my cousin too?" I ask Tia.


"No, not at all. He was…" She looks for the right word, "student to your grandfather."

***

We arrive back at Tia's exhausted. I can safely add surfing to the list of sports in which I totally suck. RJ and Nat got up to a standing position a couple times, and my son even rode a small wave without wiping out. I nearly drowned twice and somehow briefly popped my shoulder out of place. The pain is killing me. Tia's looking for some tylenol, and Nat's making me an ice pack.

I carefully unroll the drawing of my Natalia. I know I will cherish this drawing for the rest of my life. At 13, she's on the precipice of major change. She's constantly told she too young for this, too old for that. She's got a big, scary, awesome adventure ahead of her and I was so happy to have captured a piece of that, forever.

I feel better after Tia fashions me a sling from a beautiful scarf. She tells me it was my Abuela's and I should keep it. I let my finger slide up and down the silky fabric. The mother of my mother had excellent taste. I ask Tia Marianna to tell me more about her and and listen for the next hour or so as she describes a woman I would have been proud to know.

It turns out my grandmother was born in abject poverty. She was the fourth of six children and they all lived in a hut with a dirt floor, in a small village 30 miles from here. Her mother, my great-grandmother, was indigenous Taíno and her father was a expatriated Cubano sailor, who only came around to get her pregnant every year or so. Abuela Natalia left home at 13 to find work in Rincon. It was at her job washing dishes in a cafe that she met Rafeal Mercado. They were married six weeks later.

Rafeal encouraged her to work, an uncommon practice back then. She moved from dishwasher to chef, eventually earning the position of head chef at one of Rincon's finest restaurants - again ahead of her time. She was writing a cookbook when her only son and youngest child, my uncle Angelo, was murdered.

I knew everything about his death. It caused my grandparents to drink themselves to their graves and started my mother's drinking problem. He was 17, a cashier at a gas station and was shot, execution-style, over less than 20 dollars in the cash register. My mother always called him her 'angel' and never recovered from his death or the related deaths of her parents. She ran away from her family, away from her homeland, and never looked back.

Tia says she needs to prepare dinner and I follow to her sunny, tiled kitchen. I am determined to learn Puerto Rican cooking, evidently it's in my blood.

\*\*\*

Learning about my grandfather came in pieces, here and there. I feel his presence on the property, though. He built both houses with his own hands. He poured the concrete of the large patio and signed it with his initials and year: 1961. The hand-carvings of my little temporary home were his work, too. I touch them whenever I walk by hoping to absorb some part, some essence maybe, of him.

I learned about Tia Marianna a little at a time as well. She was Abuela Natalia's youngest sister and had lived with her and Rafeal since she was 9-years-old. She loved my mother and my uncle like they were her own children. She worked in kitchens and as a housekeeper at the resorts until she married a man named Jose when she was 20. Jose was a commercial fisherman that died at sea a few weeks after their first anniversary. His death left her with a little money and the no desire to ever marry again.

She has lived alone here, at the Mercado Estate, for over 30 years. She rented out the guest house and relied on interest from her savings to support herself. Although Rafeal Mercado had an extensive family, as I'm learning, he left everything to my mother. She refused it and gave it all to Tia Marianna. Getting to know my great aunt also solved one of my life's great mysteries: her middle name is Joelys. I can't imagine why my mother never told me this. I have no idea why she was so incredibly secretive about her life in Rincon.

I had always imagined my mother's journey being one of great struggle and hardship. I imagined her family as destitute and drunken louts. I pictured Tijuana-like shanties. My mother threw away paradise to live in a place where the sun only comes out enough to tease. I thought of all the times we struggled; the winter we had power shut off and could see our breath in the kitchen; the trailer park I called home until I was seven; the free-lunch tickets I sheepishly gave the lunch ladies, the Goodwill clothing; the constant, debilitating fear I still have of when my next paycheck is coming; I thought of all these things and wondered why my mother gave all this away.

She was, for once, quiet.

She'd been quiet most of this trip, actually. Sure, she didn't like that I was attracted to that artist at the market and she made fun my attempt at surfing, but for the most part, I was alone in my thoughts. I wondered if I was finally starting to heal.

I knew I wasn't being haunted. I knew it wasn't the beginning of schizophrenia, or some permanently damaging mental illness. Intellectually, I knew my fractured brain had made some interesting pathways in my grief and guilt. I had done some research and diagnosed myself with something called Unwanted Thought Syndrome. It is atypical for the thoughts to come with another persona, but not unheard of. The only effective course of treatment, from what I'd read, was cognitive therapy (pass) and anti-anxiety meds (hard pass). I've decided to live with it until I somehow learn how to deal or until it became too much to bear.

## Chapter 24: American Prudishness

"Forgive me father, for I have sinned. That's what I'm supposed to say, right?" What in actual fuck am I doing?

*Do it. Tell the priest what you have done. Give him a heart attack!*

Tia Marianna looked so shocked and sad when I said we wouldn't join her for services this morning. She's been so kind, so warm and giving; I couldn't let her down. The kids looked at me like I was an alien. We could survive this I assured them. It's part of the cultural experience.

When Tia pushed me into the confession booth, I was resisting so hard I almost made a scene. I did almost everything I was asked. I genuflected, I gave greetings of peace to the neighbors, I listened to the sermon with grace and patience and didn't roll my eyes once. I was impressed with the carvings and art. The cathedral is gorgeous. I did not cross myself with water or take Holy communion. I'm not baptised; I'm not allowed. I can't believe the woman would think it appropriate for me to give confession.

"It's hot in this booth. You should have a fan." I tell the man. My ass is glued to the wooden bench. I should have worn panties.

"We make due." He chuckles. "You're not from around

here."

"No. I'm visiting my aunt. She made me sit in here. Can we just chit chat a few minutes so I can say I did it?"

"Sure, my child. Is there anything you'd like to talk to about?" He's got a kind voice.

"Well, I don't suppose you'd like to get into the Church's misogynistic stance on birth control?" Hey, he asked.

"I know its stance. I tell people in my flock that God only wants the best for them. God also gave them free will and we are likely allowed to take medication that may improve our lives."

His answer impressed me and I calmed down. "You're alright, father."

"Thanks visitor. How long are you in town?"

"Three more weeks."

"Make sure you have the fish stew at Cabranino's. It'll change your life!" He shuts the little window and I try to appear somber when I walk out.

\*\*\*

After I showered the godliness off me, I rounded up the kids to play around with our new snorkels. Tia said if we went past the furthest part of the inlet, just a few more feet, there was little bit of coral and we'd see some interesting fish. I strap RJ into a life vest and we go adventuring.

The water is clear for yards ahead of us. We see the coral where Tia had directed. It's not a huge reef, clusters of grey formations with barnacles and other forms of life growing on it. A school of little, bright yellow fish appear from behind its shelter and dart between us. It's incredible, so very unique and special form anything else I'd seen. I hold tight to the kids' hands at various points, wanted to add to my tactile memory of these moments.

\*\*\*

As I was drying the water from my hair, I saw Xavier's lean frame saunter toward me. I quickly wrap the towel around me. I don't look terrible in it, but my two piece was purchased only for comfort.

"Did you enjoy your snorkeling?" He asks.

"How did you…?" I question but stop when he points down to my flippered feet. I try to kick them off quickly but end up tripping myself and falling into his arms. Great. Like something out of a damn romcom. I smile up at him cutely but his expression stays the same, shaded by his grey, vintage hat.

I right myself and ask if he's here for dinner.

"Yes. Marianna's a wonderful cook. I would never refuse her offer." He's still blank-faced, stoic. He's staring at me intently. I resist the urge to wipe my face, like maybe I have something on it.

"Well, let's head to the house, then." I start that way

but he stays put. I turn to him.

"Why did you cover up when you saw me?" He asks.

"I hardly know you and this is more skin than I'd usually show a stranger." I'm perplexed by this man's rudeness.

"I see." I nods and finally looks away. "American prudishness."

"Hey, buddy, you don't know me. I am the opposite of a prude." My voice raises with indignant contempt. How dare he! The kids are running past us or I'd have used stronger language.

"What do you care what I think?" He asks simply and heads to the house.

Xavier is subtly contemptuous toward me the whole meal. Nothing I can call him out on, or would have given my aunt's fondness for the man, but there's palpable distaste. I'm grateful that he claims to have somewhere to be and exits after the meal.

Unfortunately, he forgets his hat and Tia sends me after him. I rudely throw it to him after calling his name and turn around quickly, back toward the house.

"Have you a problem with me, Joelys?" He taunts. The way he says my name is unlike Tia's warmth. He throws the hard 'Y' sound out like a swear word, as if it's bitter in his mouth.

"Yeah, pal, I do." I turn again. "You were rude to me all night. I was excited to meet you. Somehow you were a student of my grandfather's, which I don't even understand, given that he died around the time you were born. My aunt really respects you and your art," I soften, "your art is incredible. I was looking forward to talking to you and all I got was a cold shoulder."

"There is much for you to learn, Joelys. I can't understand why you're only *now,* after all these years, visiting Marianna. She talked about you and your mother constantly. For over a decade, I heard how she was waiting for a visit or an invite to visit. She showed me pictures, I've seen every picture of you and your kids you've sent. She shows everyone, so proud! But you didn't even invite her to her nieces' funeral. She read about it in your stupid annual Christmas card!"

I'm taken aback. I don't know what to say. "You don't understand."

"Enlighten me. You want the house? Do you think there's money?" He looks disgusted with me.

"I had no idea." I'm on the verge of tears. "My mother never talked about this place. She never talked about Tia Marianna. It was too painful for her. She was a drunk and…" I try to control myself. "I didn't even know she and Marianna were close! I didn't know about this house or…" Tears slid down my cheeks. "I had this whole family and history my entire life and I just found out a week ago! I've mispronounced my own name *my whole life!* My mother didn't tell me anything! It was only after my father, the only family member I thought I had left also died, did I come here to find out for myself!"

"Oh." He says softly.

"Yeah." I try to say toughly with a sniff.

"I am sorry." He says simply and genuinely. "I misunderstood. I care about Marianna a great deal."

"So do I!" I kinda laugh. It's an understandable confusion, I suppose. He sits up on the hood of his truck and pats the space next to him. I climb up and look out at the house. He offers me a cigarette. I haven't smoked since in years but I accept. I tell him I need a drink if we're going to light these.

"I know where Marianna keeps the rum." He says as he jumps off and toward the house.

\*\*\*

After a couple rums and smokes, Xavier strokes my cheek and tell me I'm beautiful in the moonlight.

"Everyone looks great in dim lighting after some rum." I scoff.

"You're beautiful always." He gently presses his lips to mine.

\*\*\*

Our second week in Rincon was a blur of activity and fun and memories we'll always cherish. I took RJ in Tia's Jeep into the mountains to find some trouble. I dated a Jeep guy in high school; I knew how to go muddin'. RJ was thrilled, actually calling me 'awesome' and thanking me with a hug. Nat and I went some museums and a concert. Tia and I drank rum into the late hours of the night, connecting.

I didn't dread Sunday as much as I thought I would. The church is beautiful and the devoted parishioners' faith was inspiring. I didn't argue about going into the confessional.

"Forgive me father for I have...you know the drill." I laugh.

"Hello visitor!" He greets me merrily.

"Great sermon this morning." I offer. "I've always appreciated the Christian virtues of forgiveness. You teach that lesson well." I was being honest. His words moved me.

"Thank you! It's nice to get feedback - especially from cynics." He chuckles.

"I'm not a cynic, really. I'm just an atheist. I've never felt the need to allow an outside force to control my morality or how I live my life."

"Some people do. Some people need an instruction booklet. Life is really hard - especially when you don't have direction or support. The Church gives that, and much more, to many people." He speaking softly, thoughtfully. I hear him shift in his seat. "Who do you need to forgive, visitor?"

"My parents." I have no reason to be guarded in this box. "My ex-husband. My son. And, to be honest, myself."

"That is a lot to carry alone. Thank you for trusting me with a piece of your burden." His words aren't preachy or weighted. He's a genuine, kind man. In this moment, I'm grateful Tia pushed me in here.

"How do you let go, Father?" It comes out as a rough, broken whisper.

"You're not going to like my answer. You let go through faith." He pauses, but I don't say anything. I knew the divinity stuff would come up. "I have faith in God. You'll need to do as you've always done and have faith in yourself. Trust that you're capable of letting it go and try."

I draw a long, deep breath and thank the man. He closes our conversation with a recommendation of a pastry shop.

***

Xavier and I went out twice this week. He took me for the clergy-approved fish stew and we went dancing at a salsa club. I finally found an activity my body was made for! I would definitely find a salsa dance class back home. We'd shared a few kisses and he was constantly reciting Spanish poetry to me, but we hadn't seen each other naked. I wanted to, but I also didn't want him or Tia thinking I was an easy or cheap woman.

*I thought you were proud of being a whore! My daughter, the girl no shame!*

I really liked the man. He wasn't what I usually went

for, macho and rugged, or whatever it was I usually sought. Aside from his extraordinary talent, Xavi is smart and soft-spoken and passionate.

I'd promised myself I wouldn't have any flings or casual fucks while I was here with my kids. I wanted them to get my 100% attention. But they were as encouraging as my aunt when he asked me out. They liked Xavier. RJ even sat for a portrait while they talked about soccer. Tia Marianna was more than happy to push me out the door. She said she and the kids needed me to leave so they could make some secrets of their own.

***

I had business to attend to here and I was avoiding it. I'd carefully packed my mother's and father's ashes. I'd planned on doing it right away, but lost my nerve.

***

Nat and I went to the market to get some items for Tia and bring Xavier some lunch and cookies. Looking out at the crowd, I realized something. I fit in here.

Everywhere I looked, I saw women of all ages in low-cut, short dresses. The women wear vivid colors and bold patterns. They have big asses and even bigger hair. Girls of all ages and shapes show their cleavage and shapely legs. Partially, it was the heat, but everyone seemed freer with themselves.

Also, everyone is loud. No one shushes you. Everyone interrupts, it's not rude. There were people lighter-skinned than me and some darker. It wasn't an issue. In Portland, you can divide neighborhoods by race. I know I was blinded by the awe of vacation, but I felt at home. I felt like I belonged.

## Chapter 25: I Did What I Could, With What I Had

I'm in Xavi's apartment/studio, of course it's a too-cool industrial loft above a warehouse. We'd gotten street tacos and watched a cool bluesy band at a park. He wanted me to come over to sit for a portrait. He convinced me when he said he needed something to remember me by when I left. He pours us some almond liqueur and rum cocktails. They have maraschino cherries, which makes me grin like an idiot. My parents were drunks, we always had jars of the candied treats in the fridge.

I ask him what Tia meant when she said he was a student of my grandfather's. He told me I should really ask Tia Marianna that question, it's not entirely his story to tell. He tells me to sit on this tall stool by some lamps. I say I will if I can take my drink. He poses me a little and turns on half of the lights. He tells me to move very little. He steps back and shakes his head. He comes back and adjusts me again. He asks if I like the dress I'm wearing.

"Well, it's not my favorite but I think it's fi-" I'm cut off as he rips the neckline. It falls down my shoulders and exposes my breasts. He lightly bites one, kisses my lips, and tells me not to move.

Now I see why women are hot for artists.

\*\*\*

Sharing a cigarette in his bed, I can't stop looking at the drawing. It's me, clearly, but I look endlessly sexy. He didn't firm up my breasts or edit my forehead lines, but I look like a goddess. It's erotic but classy and I can't believe he sees that in me. He catches my stare and says, "I saw all that in you years ago. In the pictures Marianna showed me. I just had to wait for you."

I softly caress his inner-thigh and ask, "Worth the wait?"

He fervently kisses my neck and murmurs, "Every second."

I have to leave earlier than I'd like. I can't let the kids and Tia worry about me. I ask him if I can have the drawing and he says he'll get me a quality print. The original is all for him.

\*\*\*

I wake to RJ bouncing on the bed. It's his promised JetSki day. I found an outfit to rent us two for a reasonable rate, and give us a quick lesson. I don't even have to say anything and he bounds off to get my coffee.

It was a fantastic day at sea. RJ and I shared one and I let Nat pilot her own. We raced a school of dolphins and discovered a tiny island all our own. I let RJ drive for a while, holding onto him tightly. We bonded over the shared silence, adventure, and beauty of it all. That night, he asked Nat to take the couch, he wanted to snuggle with mommy.

\*\*\*

The kids occupied with the neighbors and their XBox, it's time for Tia Marianna and I to talk about my grandfather. I'd gathered he was some sort of artist or craftsman. He was from a founding family in Rincon, the Mercado name got me all sorts of raised eyebrows and respectful murmurs. Everyone says he was a great man, but no one gave details. I needed to know more. I can't believe my mother never talked about him.

*How much do you like to talk about your dead daddy?*

Touche, mom. But still I wanted to know more. Tia led me into a bedroom on the upper floor of the house. The door had a hand-carved plaque: "ANGELO". This must have been his room. I remembered a matching one with my mother's name in a box she kept under her bed. Not knowing it's importance, I'd given it to the Goodwill. Knowing what I know now, I'm saddened I'd not held on to it. The bedroom is packed full with boxes and bulky objects under sheets. I see glimpses of 1970s posters featuring bands and movies and cars. Under all this stuff, I bet the room is a shrine.

I see a huge, lacquered piece of wood at our feet. I angle my body to get a better look. It's old, a bit dusty but I read, "Mercado Signs".

"My grandfather had a sign shop?!" I am blown away.

"Did not your mother tell you?" Tia dismisses it. Of course, she wouldn't know the relevance to me. Why, oh why, had my mother never told me? She had to have known my interest. My passion. I could have studied under…

Oh, wait.

*Yeah, dipshit. He was dead. But you also don't remember why you had a fascination with signs. I pointed them out to you, since you were old enough to listen. I taught you to care about them and the lettering. I gave you endless pens. I did what I could, with what I had.*

The sign was amazing. The detail work had to have taken him weeks. I run my hands over the flowers in the corners. I feel tears and I don't fight them. It's like the carvings in the guest house. They show his talent and love. I feel close to the man. Tia Marianna's on the other side of the room now, unearthing some canvases.

Rafeal was an incredible talent, it appears. There's altogether 30 paintings, and each better than the last. He was of the impressionist's school, but with a daring use of color and tighter strokes. I stop dead when I get to a portrait of my mother. She looks to be about 16, in a peach gown. Before the pain, the grief, and the booze: her face was light and gay. Her crooked grin was ripe with mischief and promise. I fall to my knees in grief. Not only for the loss of her life, but the incredible losses she suffered.

"Tia?" I asked when I can breathe again. "How do you do it? How did you survive all this pain? You lost everyone too, but you're ok. You didn't become a drunk or a prostitute or a jerk. You lived through so much and you're kind and happy. How?"

"Oh, my sweet girl." She slowly kneels to embrace me. "Time heals all. But you have to let it."

Time heals everything. I touch my nose-ring, thinking about how I came to the same conclusion, all on my own. "You have to let it?" I ask, sniffling.

"Your poor mother fought with time. She no wanted to heal. She thought her pain was...tribute. I choice another way to honor my dead."

\*\*\*

That night I needed the respite of Xavi's arms. Tia suggested a campout on the beach for her and the kids. I had a Puerto Rican S'more (roasted plantains instead of marshmallows) before I left. I was sad and overwhelmed, but not out of my mind. C'mon, chocolate.

I told Javier everything I learned that day. I told him about my obsession with lettering and some pictures on my phone of my beer signs. I told him finding this connection, this potential life I could have had, hurt as much as not knowing anything. He let me vent, stroked my hair, and gave me supportive kisses when he felt I needed them. He told me I was talented and I accepted the praise. It meant a lot to me that he, this great artist, thought so.

After some quiet he told me how his uncle had one of my grandfather's paintings in his home. As a little boy, Xavi was obsessed with the piece. He studied it for hours and tried to recreate it with crayons. When he got paints and some lessons, it was over for the boy. He knew where he belonged. After art school in the states, he returned home. He looked up Rafeal Mercado and found my aunt. The two became friends and she let Xavier borrow or have whatever he wanted from what was left of my grandfather's art. She supported his budding career and let him live in the guest house for free.

I tell him about the carving and engraving supplies I'd inherited today, a box of obviously loved chisels, spacing rulers, and exacting tools. There were a few educational books in the box, too. I asked if Javier carved and could maybe teach me a bit. He denied any talent for it, but could show the basics. In the morning, of course. We currently had important business to attend to: namely his erection pressed to my side.

\*\*\*

In the morning, I slipped in before the kids started to stir in the fort they'd constructed. I made the coffee for Tia and plated the pastries I had picked up on the way. The lady at the panaderia y reposteria grinned at me in my clearly walk-of-shame outfit and hair. There was no shame, though. She was happy for me. Puerto Ricans aren't afraid of their sexuality, at least not in Rincon.

*Yeah, yeah. Tell them about your coke and johns. See how evolved they are then!*

I change quickly and throw my hair on top of my head, in the style of aunt. I picked up more postcards the other day, and sit to fill them out for my family back home while I sip my coffee. I express that I miss them, but can't describe how happy I am here. I promise them stories and hint to ladies there's a man involved. Tia Marianna slowly makes her way to the patio table and tells me she's too old for forts. I sympathize and thank her, pouring out a cup for this saint of a woman.

"You look happy, Joelys."

"Tia, I can't express how happy you and this magic place make me. I want to come back every summer!"

"You," She places her soft hand on mine, "my dear girl, are always welcome. This is your home."

Home. I'm overcome again. This is home. Portland is home too. It's time to start thinking about how to carry this peace with me when I return.

\*\*\*

The extended family is coming again. I now know they are mostly Mercados, but none are direct, non-removed family to me. Rafeal had no siblings, but was close to his cousins. There was one family from my grandmother's side, but again a cousin. All of Tia and Abuela's siblings had already passed. I sketched out a huge family tree, hoping to fill in the rest this evening. Tia Marianna and I went early to the market to get a small roasting pig, while the kids and Xavier readied the pit. Originally, the big party was planned for our last full day on the island. However, I asked to move it up. Turns out, the kids and I aren't the best travelers, and I want our last day to be relaxing and quiet.

The butcher is a wide, loud man, shamelessly flirting with my aunt. She tells him to knock it off, that her niece is the one buying and we all laugh. When we leave, I notice she's got a wiggle in her walk.

"Tia? Why did you not date after your husband died? You were so young." I'd been curious.

"Who say I did not?" She winks. I smile and she continues. "You were married. Did you enjoy it?"

"Sometimes." I say judiciously.

"There are people, like my sister and your mother," She crosses herself lightly, so subtle I almost missed it. "They are happy as wife to one man. Some people, like you and me are made to have many loves." Holy crap! My Tia's a progressive genius!

*She said many loves, not many dicks.*

\*\*\*

At the party, I catch Nat and a boy kissing on the far side of the guest house. I'd only ventured over there for a private place to make out with Xavier. We see the two and hide quickly. I had no idea she was even interested in boys yet. I peek again, just to try to identify the level of cousin she's picked and see it's one of the neighbor's sons.

Xavi and I run back to the party. He asks if I'm ok with what I'd seen. I'm weirdly at peace. She's growing up; this is a natural step for her. Of course the daughter of Joelys Jeffries will come back from her summer vacation with a steamy story for her friends.

## Chapter 26: Adios, mi amores

Our last week in paradise was filled with adventure and love as those preceding it. I created a lifetime's worth of memories and lay here, this morning, thanking every star that aligned to bring us to this place. Nat and I parasailed. RJ surfed a huge wave and found a shark's tooth. Xavi and I made love on the beach and he got me started with my carving and engraving lessons. Tia taught me all her favorite recipes and helped me package a great deal of my grandparents' belongings to ship back home.

I am not looking forward to the next couple days. Today, I will spread my parent's ashes and tomorrow, long before the sun rises, Xavi is driving us to the airport.

I sit at the patio table for my last sun-filled coffee with my great aunt. I hug her before I sit, not wanting to let a minute pass before I leave without showing her my gratitude and love. She pours and asks if I'm ready for today's events. I say I'm as ready as I'll ever be. She knew my struggles with the finality of the act. Today was my last chance to say what I needed to say, to feel what I needed to feel. I sip my coffee and mentally prepare. She holds my hand and allows me the space to think.

The graves of Rafeal, Natalia, and Angelo Mercado are in a cemetery behind the church. I've got mom's ashes in their airtight plastic packaging and metal clips to reseal the bag after I pour some out. I have planned to spread half of them here, as requested.

The other half will be combined with dad's on the shore of the Mercado inlet.

Tia Marianna, RJ, Nat, and I are all dressed as somber as the weather would allow. I study the modest headstones. Simple but gorgeous, engraved in white marble. I recognize some braiding technique on Angelo's and realize my Abuelo carved it himself. I melt into grief at even the thought of burying your own child. Today, I bring this small, broken family some closure. Well, I will when I find a damn knife.

I can't believe I thought to bring something to reseal the bag, but not something to open it! We send Nat and RJ to the church to see if the priest is around and has a cutting device we can borrow. They return with the man, fully outfitted in the his collar and everything. He greets me with, "Hola, visitor."

"Hello, Father. Thanks for the rescue. And everything else." He embraces Tia while I speak.

"No problem. Would you like me to offer a prayer for the service, as it were?"

I'm hesitant, but Tia looks thrilled. I nod. The man says something in poetic Spanish, crossing himself several times. I watch Tia Marianna's face, tense with emotion until she shares an 'Amen' with the father. He nods to me and hands me the scissors.

I cut the corner of the bag carefully. I hand the scissors back to the man and face the group.

"My mother always had one foot painfully in her past. I am happy to put her to rest, here, at her home, with her family. All of these people were taken too soon." I breathe deeply and keep my voice even. "But the impact they left on those who love them runs deep and will last an eternity."

I start pouring, slowly, deliberately. "Be at peace, mom." The others repeat my simple request. Be at peace, sobrina. Be at peace, grandma.

Be at peace, mom.

\*\*\*

I told the others I needed to do the rest on my own. We agree that after I spread them, everyone will take their own time and space to say good-bye as they desire. I decide to open and pour out the bag of what was left of my father first. Because of his health concerns, coupled with how suddenly we lost mom, dad and I said what we needed to say to each other. I never shied from an opportunity to spend time with him or share my feelings. I was somewhat prepared for his death, as much as a person can be. I cut the bag and wave it over the shore, letting the contents fly free. I watch the last of the floating particles settle.

"I love you, daddy." The tears start. Gasping sobs escape my mouth. I don't have to be brave for anyone. I allow myself to let go.

"Thank you for loving me and teaching me. Thank you for always having my back. Thank you for showing me what it is to be a good person. I love you forever, dad. I miss you every single day. Mom's coming soon." After a few moments of watching the dry ash soak into the ocean's salty water, I blow a kiss toward them. I used to blow my daddy a kiss every night when he turned off my bedroom light.

After I calm, I sit on my towel with my bag. I've got a bottle of rum and two glasses. I situate the rest of mom's ashes across from me and pour us each a drink. I raise mine to the expansive horizon and take a sip.

"So, mom, we need to talk."

*What, so you can tell me what a terrible mother I was? Go ahead, get your closure.*

I take another drink. "I've got to let you go, mom. I can't believe it's taken me this long to understand, but I'm angry with you."

*No shit, Sherlock. ¡Estúpida!*

"Not for what I thought, though. Mom, you killed yourself. You left me. We could have had so many more years together and you took that away from me."

I sip. "You devastated me and dad. I understand that you were in pain. I understand, now more than ever, you saw no other way. But I need you. I needed my mommy. My life fell apart and the worst thing was how alone I felt without you."

*I'm sorry, mija. I know. I'm really sorry I wasn't stronger for you.*

"I forgive you, mom." I take a big drink. "I forgive you for your imperfections. I forgive you for leaving me too soon. I forgive you for keeping all this," I gesture at the surroundings, "from me. I forgive you." I say the last part loudly, in case somehow she actually could hear me on some level.

"It's time to let go." I say to myself as much as her and stand up. I finish the drink and reopen the bag of her ashes.

I shake the contents out in the same place, the same way I had with my father.

"I love you mommy. Thank you for teaching me to stand up for myself. Thank you for showing me how to be strong. Thank you for loving me, no matter what. Thank you for taking care of me when I was sick and brushing my hair." I'm sobbing again, without restraint. "I love you so much, mom. I miss you and will honor you every day. You and daddy are free now. You're together, where you belong."

I pick up the other rum and gulp half the glass. This is how the Jeffries pray. I then pour the rest on ground in memorial. I stand for a while, gathering myself and watching the waves. The tide's coming in: proof of the unending cycle of how the world - despite our pain or grief, despite how often we wish for something different - it keeps turning.

\*\*\*

Our final night in Rincon, at least for this summer, is spent eating a simple dinner of finger foods: cured meats, cheeses, pickled vegetables, and rolls; on the outdoor table and sharing laughter and tears. I'm a wreck, but somehow clearer and more focused than I'd felt in ages. My brain was a sidewalk after a torrential rain, clean and fresh. I made plans with Tia for Christmas. She'd never seen snow before, so we were planning to fly her to Portland.

Xavier and a couple of the cousins I'd grown close to, two women about my age, were also in attendance. The women, Ana and Florencia, helped me pack and tidy the guest house. Florencia's mother and my mother were best friends growing up. Unfortunately, the woman had passed away as well, but Flor had some stories to share. Ana was to wed next summer and I promised to try to come. I winked at her, making a crack about how if I was engaged to such a handsome man I'd just elope. I saw them off, and checked my list.

Xavier says it's weird how I'm hyper organized and pure chaos. I smile and say I got the best of both my parents. I wait for my mother to say something indignant about how I'm not at all like her but there's nothing. Silence. He asks what I'm thinking about.

"Your dumb, handsome face." I lie, stealing a kiss.

"I notice you only invited your Tia for visits?" Ha half asks, half hints, pulling me tightly against him. "I am just your summer fling?"

This is the moment. Where we try to make some sort of plans to see each other again, to ask him to move, to make some sweeping declarations.

"You're my Puerto Rican love." I say. "I adored every second we shared and hope to see you next time I visit."

"What, I'm supposed to wait here, pining for you every day for a year?" He's kisses my cheek.

"No, of course not. You'll live, you'll create, you'll flirt with pretty tourists. You'll be happy. And I'll be happy. And when I come back, if you're free and I'm free, we know how to find each other."

"And if I'm not? If I find someone else with a beautiful face and a laugh that makes my heart leap?" He looks a little hurt, but I think it's more about damaged ego.

"Then I will be sad for my loss but happy for someone I love to have found that." I kiss him again. "What we have is special and rare. The duration does not define it."

He shows acceptance by swinging me around and pulling my back into him, kissing my neck. "You promise to visit next summer?"

\*\*\*

Our trip home was long but uneventful. No chance encounters with old flames or sketchy taxicabs. We arrive at PDX to a little fanfare from Gene. He's been house sitting and taking care my asshole cat. He did a funny bit where he pretended not to recognize me, it had been so long. I laughed and hugged my dear friend tight. He asked for all the crazy details but accepted that my tired brain just needed some quiet at the moment. The kids fell asleep the minute they were buckled. I watch the rain hit the highway as we move, the drops splashing back so hard it looks as if the road was returning fire.

## Chapter 27: Happy Endings (tee hee)

Jason's at the lathe, showing RJ how to finish and buff the bindle with fine sandpaper. The two work well together, both quietly determined to learn. The workshop is expansive but efficient. I watch them from a commercial printer, waiting for it to finish. Nat's here too, organizing the materials for the boys. I look out the window to the judge the intentions of the November sky.

I can't believe it's November already. In a few days it'll be the anniversary of my father's death. I'm not making a big deal about it. Just tacos and a couple beers with good friends.

I check my phone, anxious. I know that Gene is proposing to Allie sometime today. It's probably not anytime soon, likely over dinner. I'm still super excited to add one more to the family. I tell Jason I've got to move my Jeep. The one thing that sucks about this place: parking. But that's everywhere in The City of Roses. RJ asks to come and I grin. You know how some guys buy a real nice car, calling it a 'babe magnet'? I traded in the caddie for this old, rugged Jeep to get closer to my son. And I have zero regrets.

We're better than ever, RJ and me. I've found a peace in his choice to live with his dad. I didn't lose my son. I didn't do anything wrong. I allowed him to make a decision for his happiness, and someday that's the part he'll remember. Mom loved him and respected him enough to let him make the choice. And he'll remember our adventures into the

mountains, climbing impossible hills and getting dirty.
We move the Jeep to a coveted, non-metered spot
across the street and he hops out, excited to ride
even that tiny distance.

Things are great in pretty much every aspect of my
life. I've found work that fulfills me. My children are
growing into creative, independent people and we've
bonded in ways I'd never imagined. My friends are
still my family by choice and we treat each other
extraordinarily well. My mother is at peace and no
longer haunting my thoughts. I've found the strength
to let go and forgive - even myself. I honor my dead
every day by choosing happiness.

We get back to the shop and I tell him to go in without
me. I want a moment to check out the sign. About five
feet above me, a giant wooden slab is secured to the
brick building. MERCADO SIGNS, in perfectly carved
slab lettering. I've added turquoise and hot pink
highlighting to make the dark wood pop. It's retro,
funky, and artisan: perfect for the buyers in the area.
It was a small fortune to ship, but worth every penny
to me. Mercado Signs lives again.

I've also painted our other services on the storefront
window in a fun, eye-catching way. We specialize in
handcrafted or painted signs, menus, advertisement
boards, and banners. We also custom engrave and
embroider. We make trophies, awards, and pet
collars. We print and copy. We'll pretty much make
you anything you can imagine. We rent out our
equipment as a maker's space, after hours to people
who subscribe monthly. I purchased the heavy
equipment slightly used: the ink printer, the 3D printer,
the engraver, the compressor, and the woodworking

supplies. I got screaming deal on the lot from a maker's space that went under in Seattle. I felt confident in my business model, unlike the guy who folded, because my commercial lease was shockingly affordable and we offer more services.

Handmade signage is trendy right now. Since I opened, I haven't had a day without an order coming in for some hipster bullshit menu or sandwich board. I'd also secured a contract with two school districts for trophies and plaques. We've been operational for almost a month and while we're not making a fortune, we're turning a tiny profit. It's too new for us to speculate, but I literally bet a quarter of my fortune that we'll succeed.

Jason came on board as soon as I pitched it. I needed his carpentry skills and support. Luck was on my side, his hours would be seasonally cut with Dave's construction outfit and he had the time. We were completely over the weirdness of my sexual advances and his crush. He was the brother I always wanted, a powerful and meaningful addition to my life and to my heart. We had a blast setting this place up. We made puns and tongue-in-cheek jokes on the displays. There's an award for 'Oral Excellence' made out to a famous porn star, and a plaque from the law offices of Dewey, Cheatum & Howe.

I walk into my shop with a renewed pride in ownership. I'd just received a letter from Tia Marianna this morning, gushing about how proud she was of my bravery. Hanging a shingle isn't a small thing; it takes guts. I wasn't too worried about it. I always seem to find a way to make things work. Without a degree or a work history, I've paid my mortgage on time every

month since my divorce. The kids have never gone
hungry. Clearly, I've never found an obstacle I can't
overcome. All you need is time.

\*\*\*

The bell rings and I hand my paintbrush to Nat. I wipe
my hands on my apron and see a tall, handsome man
in a suit walking to the counter. He says he's here to
pick up a plaque and hands me the order number. I
yell back to have Nat grab it and smile at the man,
admiring his strong jaw and Wall Street good looks.
He compliments the small menu board on the
counter, waiting for pickup. I thank him and bite my lip
a little. He asks if it's my work and I nod proudly.

Completing his transaction, I give him my business
card with his order and receipt. I thank him and he
asks if my cell is listed.

"Not yet." I say with a wink, scribing it on the back. He
leaves with a sexy nod and I grin.

I mean, I may be all healthy and healed and happy or
whatever - but I'm always going to be me.